Seth had seen hard emotions in her eyes before, but this was a storm of a different kind.

A storm that he was going to have to stop before Shelby made up her mind to do something stupid.

So, he leaned in and kissed her.

A smart man would have come up with something a whole lot better, but Seth suddenly wasn't feeling very smart in that department. Heck, maybe he just wanted to kiss her. And it seemed to work. Shelby stopped talking about a deadly showdown and slipped right into his arms.

It obviously wasn't the first time Seth had kissed her, but like the other times, he felt that kick of surprise. Surprise that anyone could taste this good. Or feel this way in his arms.

Yeah, stupid.

Because kissing Shelby wasn't doing a thing to help them out of their dangerous situation.

A LAWMAN'S JUSTICE

—

USA TODAY Bestselling Author
DELORES FOSSEN

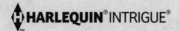

HHARLEQUIN® INTRIGUE®

Recycling programs
for this product may
not exist in your area.

ISBN-13: 978-0-373-74902-7

A Lawman's Justice

Printed in U.S.A.

Delores Fossen, a *USA TODAY* bestselling author, has sold over fifty novels with millions of copies of her books in print worldwide. She's received the Booksellers' Best Award and the RT Reviewers' Choice Best Book Award, and was a finalist for a prestigious RITA® Award. You can contact the author through her webpage at dfossen.net.

Books by Delores Fossen

Harlequin Intrigue

Sweetwater Ranch

Maverick Sheriff
Cowboy Behind the Badge
Rustling Up Trouble
Kidnapping in Kendall County
The Deputy's Redemption
Reining in Justice
Surrendering to the Sheriff
A Lawman's Justice

The Lawmen of Silver Creek Ranch

Grayson
Dade
Nate
Kade
Gage
Mason
Josh
Sawyer

Visit the Author Profile page
at Harlequin.com for more titles.

CAST OF CHARACTERS

FBI agent Seth Calder—This cowboy-agent wants to clear his stepmother of murder charges, but his investigation leads him to old secrets, new lies and a dangerous attraction to the woman he considers his enemy.

Shelby Braddock—An investigative reporter whose search for the truth puts her on a collision course with Seth and with a killer who wants to silence her.

Whitt Braddock—Shelby's father, who was murdered twenty-three years ago, but who really killed him?

Jewell McKinnon—Seth's stepmother. She's in jail awaiting trial for Whitt's murder. All the evidence points to her, but Jewell's not talking.

Roy McKinnon—Jewell's ex-husband who had his own motive for wanting Whitt dead.

Marvin Hance—A former FBI agent who hates Shelby because of some articles she's written about him.

Annette Prior—Whitt's former lover. Once she saw Shelby as an ally in her quest for justice, but is Annette everything that she seems to be?

Chapter One

Special Agent Seth Calder slipped his gun from his shoulder holster and stepped from his truck. He eased the door shut so the sound wouldn't alert anyone.

If there was anyone around to alert, that was.

The criminal informant who'd called him an hour earlier had said there was talk about some kind of evidence here. The CI didn't know exactly what the evidence was, but it was in an abandoned warehouse on Miller Road just outside the ranching town of Sweetwater Springs. Seth was already familiar with the warehouse, since the FBI had had it under surveillance a few months back.

Because it'd been a holding facility for a black market baby ring.

Just the thought of it put a knot in Seth's gut. The FBI and local cops had shut down the black market ring, had made plenty of arrests, too, but maybe something inside would lead to yet more arrests.

Or, God forbid, even more missing babies.

That was why Seth had gotten out here as fast as he could.

The gray metal building showed no signs of life, though. No trees within a hundred yards. And no other buildings were nearby. Just a huge concrete parking lot with weeds poking up through the cracks.

Using slow, cautious steps, Seth started toward the building but came to a quick stop when he heard an engine. The road wasn't exactly on the beaten path, so he waited and watched as the dark blue car came around the curve.

The driver hit the brakes.

Seth took a closer look. Then he cursed. What the devil was *she* doing here?

He intended to find out.

No one had ever accused him of having a friendly face when he was on the job, and Seth put on his best scowl when he walked toward Shelby Braddock's car. She didn't wait for him to reach her. She stepped out, her movements jerky and hurried, and she matched him scowl for scowl.

To say they were enemies would be like saying the ocean had a bit of water in it.

Shelby started toward him, the May breeze

flying through her dark brown hair. "Why are you here?" she snapped.

"Why are *you* here?" Seth snapped right back.

And they stood there, both glaring and waiting for the other to answer first. To remind her that he was the one in charge here, Seth tapped his badge clipped to his belt.

Her eyes narrowed. "You're pulling the FBI card on me? Well, it won't work. I'm not leaving here until I have some answers."

Seth didn't normally have it in for investigative reporters. On occasion a few actually had helped the FBI with active cases. But he had it in for this particular one. Shelby was a thorn in his thorn-riddled side.

"Exactly what kind of answers are you hoping to get here?" he asked. And yeah, it sounded like an interrogation question that he would aim at a hostile suspect.

"Obviously the same answers you're hoping to get."

Seth's scowl got worse. They had another staring match before Shelby huffed.

"I got an anonymous call, all right?" she grumbled finally. "The person said there was evidence here connected to your stepmother's trial, and I wanted to find out if that was true."

Well, hell. Seth hadn't expected *that* answer. But it was true that his stepmother, Jewell, was just three days away from standing trial. For murder.

That didn't help his churning stomach, either.

Jewell had been charged with killing her alleged lover twenty-three years ago. It'd taken all these years for the arrest to happen, and one of the main reasons for Jewell's arrest was standing right in front of him.

Shelby.

She'd written dozens of scathing articles about what she called a police cover-up, and the articles had caught the eye of the new prosecutor, who'd reopened the case. The evidence had been retested, new evidence found.

And the new evidence all had pointed to his mother being a killer.

Seth was 1000 percent sure Jewell was innocent, but so far he'd had zero luck proving it.

Until now, that was. Maybe this was the break he needed if there was indeed something in the building.

"What kind of evidence?" Seth demanded.

Shelby lifted her hands, palms up. "That's what I'm here to find out. Now, why are you here?"

Seth debated whether he should tell her, but there was no logical reason why she shouldn't know, though he could think of a few petty ones. He decided to put the pettiness aside. For now. "I got a call from a CI who said there was possibly some evidence inside. I thought it might be connected to the black market baby ring."

Her eyes widened. And Seth knew why. Both of them had received calls. His CI was as trustworthy as a criminal informant could be. Which meant the guy could be swayed by a buck or two. And Shelby's contact had been anonymous. Yet the calls had brought them here together with the lure of something they both wanted—evidence.

That couldn't be good.

"You should leave now," Seth told her, and he turned to head back to the warehouse.

Of course, she didn't leave. Shelby trailed right along behind him. "But what if there really is something inside connected to the murder investigation?" she asked.

"Then, I'll find it and turn it over to the authorities."

She huffed. Again, he knew why. Shelby likely thought he wouldn't want to add any more nails to his stepmother's coffin. But if he did indeed find something, he wouldn't suppress it. Because if Jewell was truly innocent—and Seth had to believe she was—then the total package of evidence would exonerate her.

Seth had to hope that.

"This could be dangerous," he reminded her. He hadn't figured that would get her running, and he was right. It didn't. He'd read some of the articles she'd done, and Shelby wasn't a runner. She did all sorts of risky, stupid things to get a story.

Except this wasn't just about a story.

Because Jewell had been accused of murdering Shelby's father, Whitt.

That made this personal for both of them, and even though it wouldn't stop him from looking inside the warehouse, Seth knew it was never a good idea to mix personal stuff with business.

"I'm not leaving," Shelby insisted.

Seth wanted to roll his eyes. "Then, at least stay behind me in case something goes wrong."

Of course, she didn't do that, either. Shelby got in step along beside him. So close that he caught her scent.

Something girlie.

Or maybe *womanly* was the right word.

It was some kind of shampoo mixed with something natural. Something that reminded him that Shelby was a woman and not merely a neck he'd sometimes like to wring.

Seth decided to ignore her and her scent so he could get on with his job. The sooner he did that, the sooner he could figure out if there was something to find and then get the heck out of there.

The front door to the warehouse was wide-open, but Seth didn't go there. Instead, he went to one of the windows that dotted the exterior. The glass was filmy and cracked, but he looked inside. Then he cursed under his breath.

It was too dark to see anything.

That meant going inside without the benefit of knowing if someone was lurking there, ready to attack.

"If someone shoots at us," Seth snarled, "at least show some common sense and get down so you don't get your head blown off."

He hadn't meant that to scare her. Okay, he had. But as with his other attempts, she didn't scare this time. Shelby was right on his heels when he stepped into the doorway. Seth braced himself for whatever might happen, but nothing did.

He stood there a moment so his eyes could adjust to the darkness, and then he had a look around. It was basically just one giant room with what appeared to be an office on his left and an exit straight ahead. There was another room with its door closed on the right side of the building.

Boxes and other debris were scattered around, and the place smelled like a giant dust ball. Roaches skittered across the floor. It'd been more than six months since it'd been used to house the black market babies, and it was obvious no one had cleaned it since then.

He stepped inside the building. Bracketing his

shooting wrist with his other hand, he pivoted in all directions.

Nothing.

And no sounds to indicate anyone else was inside.

Seth didn't let down his guard, though. He kept his gun ready and went to the office door. What was left of it anyway. It was hanging on just one hinge, and it squeaked and swayed a little when he moved past it.

Creepy, but no one was in the office.

Behind him he heard Shelby fumbling around, and she pulled a penlight from her back jeans' pocket. Seth took out his as well, and they clicked them on at the same time.

"If you find anything, don't touch it," Seth warned her.

She made a "duh" sound and fanned the light over the ceiling, then the floor. Seth didn't see anything suspicious, but the dozen or so boxes could have something in them. He went in the direction of the nearest one, aiming his flashlight on the floor in front of him.

And he came to a dead stop.

Oh, no. Not that.

He stooped down, garnering Shelby's attention because she hurried over to him. Seth moved the light closer so he could get a better look.

There was a plate-size area of shiny liquid on the concrete floor.

"Is that blood?" Shelby asked.

Seth didn't touch it, but it sure looked like blood to him. And it was fresh at that, with no dry spots even around the edges. He wasn't sure exactly how long it took a pool of blood that big to start drying in a hot building, but he didn't think it was hours.

More likely, minutes.

He stood, practically snapping to attention, and had another look around. Seth still didn't see anyone. Especially not someone with an injury serious enough to cause that kind of blood loss. However, a few of those boxes were large enough for someone to hide behind.

Seth kept watch around them, and he took out his phone so he could hand it to Shelby. "Call 9-1-1 and request officers on the scene."

Thankfully, she did it without hesitation or arguing. The dispatcher would direct the call to the Sweetwater Springs sheriff's office. To Seth's stepbrother, Sheriff Cooper McKinnon. And while Seth and he weren't exactly on friendly terms, he knew Cooper would do his job and get out here fast. This was likely a crime scene, and it needed to be processed.

And maybe more.

Maybe someone here needed medical attention. First, though, Seth had to find out where that someone was.

He fanned the light over the floor again. More blood. Big drops that looked as if they'd splattered from at least a few feet of distance. The drops didn't lead to the first box, but he checked it out anyway.

Nothing.

So he moved on, following the blood trail. Past all the boxes and the trash. The trail stopped right outside the room with the closed door.

Of course it did.

This couldn't be easy. That closed door could conceal the very person responsible for that blood loss. Or someone who was dying. Either way, Seth had to check it out.

He looked back at Shelby. "This would be a good time for you to go back to your car and wait for Cooper."

Her chin came up, and even with just the dim light, he saw the resolve in her eyes.

Seth could have arrested her and gotten her butt out of there. But that would take time and it'd mean a trip back to town. He really just wanted to see if anything was behind the door. Anything to do with the black market baby ring. Or his stepmother.

"Okay," Seth told Shelby when she didn't budge. "But don't say I didn't warn you."

Seth put his flashlight away to free up his hand, and he opened the door. It was pitch-black because the light from the windows didn't reach back there. Shelby did something about that. She turned her flashlight into the room.

And she gasped.

"Hell," Seth cursed.

They'd found the source of the blood, all right.

There was a mattress, the sheets stark white except for the dark red stains. And there in the center was a body. A male wearing only a pair of boxer shorts. The guy wasn't moving, and his skin was as white as the sheets.

Shelby was still holding up her flashlight, and Seth took her wrist to turn the light into the four corners of the room. No one was lurking there. So he aimed the light on the mattress. It was flat on the floor, so no one was beneath it, but he checked around all sides. As far as he could tell, no one was there.

"Don't go in the room," Seth ordered when Shelby started to move. "It's a crime scene."

And this time Shelby actually listened to him. A miracle. But she did keep her flashlight aimed at the body.

"What's that on his face?" she asked.

Since there were no indications that anyone was about to jump out at him, Seth took out his own flashlight again and leaned in closer, putting himself between Shelby and the body. He soon saw the probable cause of death.

Multiple stab wounds to the chest.

It was hard to count how many because of the blood, but there were plenty of them. Seth aimed the light on the dead guy's head, and his heart slammed against his chest.

Oh, hell.

"What's that on his face?" Shelby repeated, moving to the side so she could no doubt see better.

"A paper mask," Seth answered.

Of sorts.

It looked as if someone had enlarged a photo and then cut it out to create an image to cover the dead man's face.

"A mask?" Shelby leaned in. And she gasped again. "That's a picture of my father."

Yeah, it was. Whitt Braddock. The very man Seth's mother was accused of murdering.

"Oh, God," Shelby mumbled, and she just kept saying it. "Who'd do such a sick thing?"

Seth had to shake his head. He had no idea.

He wanted to take off the mask to see who was behind it, but he couldn't compromise any evidence that might be there. Shelby and he had perhaps compromised enough just by going inside the building. However, when he'd gotten that call from the CI, the last thing he'd expected was to find a dead body.

Seth backed up, trying to follow the same path that he'd used to get into the room so he would disturb as little of the area as possible. He bumped into Shelby, who wasn't moving. She seemed frozen. Her gaze was fixed on the body, and her mouth was trembling. She'd only been seven or eight years old when her dad had died, but this had to bring back what bad memories she had.

"They never did find my father's body," she said. More trembling and this time, it wasn't just her mouth. She sagged against him. "But the cops think he was stabbed multiple times because there was blood everywhere."

Seth was very familiar with the details. Heck, he'd memorized them.

"Come on," he told her. "We need to get out of here."

The last thing he wanted was to get into a shouting match with Cooper because Seth hadn't followed this search to the T.

When Shelby didn't budge, Seth took her by the arm to get her moving. But they only made it a few steps when he heard the plinking sound. Like something metallic falling onto the concrete. That barely had time to register in his mind when the smoke started to billow right toward them.

But it wasn't ordinary smoke.

It was tear gas.

Both Shelby and he started to cough immediately. The tear gas burned his throat and eyes. Seth tried to get them out of there, but it was hard to see anything. Hard to think, too.

Each step was an effort, but he headed straight for the door. He also kept his gun ready because someone had thrown that tear gas grenade, and that someone no doubt was lurking outside waiting to do heaven knew what to them.

Shelby and he were still several feet from the door when he heard a sound to his right. A footstep. But it was the only warning that Seth got before someone wearing a gas mask reached out and touched him with something.

The jolt went through Seth, all pain and static, and he had no choice but to drop to the floor.

Someone had used a Taser on him.

A split second later, Shelby made a sharp groaning noise and fell right next to him. Their eyes were open, gazes fixed on each other.

But neither could move.

Seth could only lie there as the footsteps came right toward them.

Chapter Two

The moment Shelby opened her eyes, the light stabbed into them, and she groaned.

Oh, mercy.

She was in a lot of pain. Her head throbbed like a toothache, her mouth was bone-dry and it took her several moments to remember why.

She'd been Tasered.

Seth, too.

Sweet heaven. That reminder got her eyes open wider, and Shelby automatically reached out her hands to fend off another attack. But no one was attacking her at the moment. And her hands didn't reach far.

That was when she noticed the ropes.

What the heck? Someone had tied her by the wrists to a wooden post.

Shelby glanced around to try to figure out what was going on. The rope was secured around a stall post in a barn. An old, rotting one from the looks of it, but not old or rotting enough that it gave way when she tugged as hard as she could. Of course, she couldn't tug that hard since her arms were weak and wobbly, like the rest of her.

Where was she?

Sunlight speared through holes in the ceiling and hit the floor like mini spotlights on a stage. But other than the holes and the disrepair, it could have been any old barn. She certainly didn't recognize it.

A sound quickly caught her attention. It was a hoarse groan, and she looked behind her to see Seth. Not his usual cocky self, either. He, too, was tied to a wooden post in the hay-strewn stall, and he looked as dazed as Shelby felt.

Another groan and Seth fully opened his eyes. He blinked hard, and it took him a moment to focus. However, he grumbled some profanity when his gaze finally landed on her face. Despite his wrists being tethered with the rope, he reached for his gun.

It wasn't there.

He was still wearing his shoulder holster, but it was empty.

Other than the missing gun, they were fully clothed. Seth even had on his Stetson.

"Where are we?" he asked but didn't wait for an answer. "And how the hell did we get here?"

Shelby had to shake her head on both counts,

and she again pulled at the thick ropes to see if they'd give way. They didn't. So she struggled some more. The wood creaked a little, but it held.

"I remember hitting the floor at that warehouse," she said when Seth repeated his questions. Good grief, her mouth felt as if she'd eaten a bag of cotton balls, and her heart was racing from the new jolt of adrenaline she'd just gotten. "What about you? What's the last thing you remember?"

He pulled in a hard breath. "Same here— nothing after someone hit me with the Taser."

Of course, before that she remembered the dead body on the mattress with the mask covering his face. Not just any mask, but a likeness of her father. She got another jolt. Not of adrenaline this time but a sickening knot in the pit of her stomach from the memories.

Shelby didn't think she'd ever forget seeing that body. That mask. All that blood.

Obviously someone had killed the man.

But who?

And why hadn't the same person killed Seth and her?

There must have been plenty of opportunities to do just that once they'd been unconscious. So why had the person left them alive and tied them up like this?

Too many questions and not nearly enough answers. Or time. Shelby had no idea where their captor was, but she figured it wouldn't be long before he came to check on them. They needed to be gone by then.

"Do you see anyone?" Seth asked.

Shelby had looked around when she first regained consciousness, but she did it again. "No one." She craned her neck so she could get a glimpse through the partially open door. "I don't see a vehicle, either."

Though someone had brought them here in some kind of vehicle. The warehouse wasn't close to any barns, so their captor would have had to drive them here. Drag them to the vehicle, too. That explained why her body felt like one giant bruise and why she had scrapes on her hands and knees.

"Someone must have drugged us," Seth told her.

Yes, that had to be it. Unfortunately, the person must have done that right after they were Tasered. Shelby didn't remember being drugged, but she did recall someone stepping around them in those moments after the initial attack. She'd also felt a stinging sensation in her arm, perhaps from someone injecting drugs into her.

"The person had on boots," she said.

Seth nodded. "And green cargo pants. I didn't

get a look at his face because he was wearing a gas mask, but it was definitely a man. He had beefy hands."

Shelby didn't recall the hands part or the gas mask, but something else popped into her head. "I don't think he was alone."

"He wasn't." Seth's forehead bunched up as if he was trying to recall the details through the fog that the stun gun and drugs had created. "I think someone came in through the back exit."

That made sense because it wouldn't have been easy for just one person to move two adults. Especially Seth. He was at least six foot three, and solid. Plus, while unconscious, Seth and she would have been dead weight.

Sweet heaven. What else had their captors done to them?

Seth began to yank at the ropes, but he didn't have any better luck getting out of them or snapping the wood than she had. He struggled several more seconds and then patted his jeans' pockets. The ones he could reach anyway.

And he shook his head.

"No phone. What about you?" he asked.

Shelby's head was still so foggy that she hadn't even considered making a 9-1-1 call. She couldn't reach her jeans' pocket, but she leaned her hip to the side so she could feel it when she pressed down onto the floor. But she also had to shake her head.

"My phone's gone," she answered. "Flashlight and car keys, too."

So the person behind this wasn't just a killer but a kidnapper and a thief, as well. Of course, he'd probably taken the flashlight and keys so she couldn't use them as pseudo weapons. Whoever was behind this also would have taken their phones to prevent them from calling for help.

And it'd worked.

"I have a small knife all the way in the bottom of my front pants' pocket," Seth said, moving around. "I guess they didn't find it when they searched us. Any chance you can reach it?"

She had more room between the rope and her hands than Seth did, but still it wasn't enough to reach all the way back to him. Not with a foot of space between them. So Shelby started inching back on her butt while Seth maneuvered himself toward her.

They collided. Her head bopping into his face. It stung, but at least they were closer now.

Seth levered himself up to his knees, as far as he could go, and he thrust his hip in the direction of her hand. She could barely reach the pocket so she kept twisting and turning until she could get her fingers inside.

"Sorry," Shelby said when her fingers slipped

in the wrong direction. She definitely hadn't wanted to touch him *there*.

He dismissed it with a manly sounding grunt, but their gazes met. She saw the discomfort in his cool blue eyes. Of course, there were a lot of reasons for his discomfort other than just her touch, but the unwanted effect from the physical contact certainly hadn't helped matters.

Shelby finally located the knife and tried to clamp her fingers around it. The surface was smooth and it slipped a few times, but she worked it out of his pocket. She nearly dropped the darn thing, but she trapped it against Seth's stomach with her hand.

He took over from there even though it involved yet more touching.

Now Shelby was the one who grunted when the back of his hand collided with her breast. No apology. He just kept working, and he used his thumb to pop out the blade.

"I'll have to try to free you first," he insisted. "The angle's wrong for me to cut through my own rope."

Suddenly, the little two-inch pocketknife blade looked as big and sharp as a switchblade, but Shelby held out her hands. Seth didn't waste a second. He started sawing while he fired glances all around them. No doubt looking for any sign of their captors returning.

It took a team effort. Seth sliced the knife back and forth while Shelby rocked in rhythm to the blade so that it would do the job faster. She was certain time wasn't on their side.

Finally, the knife cut through, and Shelby nearly toppled over as the rope fell from her wrists. She quickly righted herself, took the knife from Seth and started to cut him loose.

"I guess you aren't behind this?" he asked.

It took her a moment to realize exactly what he was asking. "You think I murdered someone in the warehouse and then stun gunned, kidnapped and drugged myself?"

He lifted his shoulder. "I was Tasered and kidnapped, too," Seth reminded her. "I know you want my mother convicted of killing your father and would do pretty much anything to see that happen. I also know you hate me."

She couldn't argue with the part about wanting Jewell to be punished for what she'd done to Shelby's father. But the second part? Well, Shelby could take some issue with that.

"I don't hate you," she corrected. "But you're not somebody I feel warm and fuzzy about."

Except for all that touching. That had certainly felt a little warm. Something that she'd carry to the grave, because Shelby had no intentions of admitting it to anyone. Especially Seth.

"I suspect you have the same non–warm and fuzzy feelings about me," Shelby added.

He didn't agree or disagree with that. He made a sound that could have meant anything or nothing. "I just want to make sure that neither you nor the trial had anything to do with this."

That evaporated any trace and memory of a warm feeling from the touching. Yes, he was talking to her as if she was a suspect.

"I can't speak for the trial, but *I* had nothing to do with this," she said through clenched teeth. "Did you?"

He gave her that flat look, the one only an FBI agent could manage. "I'm the law," he reminded her.

"And the stepson of the woman you'd like to see out of jail."

There. If he was going tit for tat, then she'd remind him that he had as much motive for this fiasco as she did.

Which wasn't much of a motive at all.

Good grief. She'd had a few verbal run-ins with Seth in the past seven months since he'd moved to the Sweetwater Ranch to be near his mother for the upcoming murder trial. But during those run-ins, he'd never accused her of multiple felonies.

"I'm an investigative reporter," she snapped. "Not a criminal like your stepmother."

That probably stung. Had to. Because from all accounts Seth loved Jewell, and some members of her family, Seth included, were likely getting desperate with the trial just days away. Well, Shelby was getting desperate, too, because she'd waited twenty-three years to get justice for her father.

She hoped her scowl conveyed that to Seth.

Shelby was so caught up in her little mental temper tantrum and scowling that she made a sound of surprise when the knife finally cut through the rope. She barely had time to move back before Seth snatched the knife from her and started toward the door. She got to her feet and hurried after him.

He stopped at the door and looked outside, but with the way he was standing, Shelby couldn't see anything except the sky. The sun was bleached white, almost blinding, and she had to blink hard several times to stop her eyes from stinging.

"Let's go," Seth whispered.

That was it, all the warning she got before he stepped out still gripping the knife. It wasn't much, but it was better than nothing.

She'd been right about the vehicles. None was in sight. But there were a rusted-out tractor, an old watering trough and what was left of a single-story, weathered gray house. It was obvious that it'd been a while since anyone had lived there.

"You recognize this place?" he asked.

"Afraid not." But she had no idea how long Seth and she had lost consciousness. Their captors would have had plenty of time to drive them pretty much anywhere, including out of the county.

Seth pulled her behind the tractor, stopped and lifted his head to listen. Shelby did the same, but the only things she heard were some birds chirping and her own heartbeat drumming in her ears. Definitely no sounds of cars, which meant there probably wasn't a main road nearby.

But there was a gravel road leading away from the place.

"There are some fresh tracks," Seth said, going closer to have a look at them.

"Should we just follow this road and see where it goes?" she asked.

"We'll follow it, but we'll have to stay out of sight. These guys will be back for us any minute now."

Shelby already had come to the same conclusion, but it made her heart beat faster to hear it confirmed.

They went off the road and onto the side away from the barn, where there were a few trees and some bushes. Nothing that would give them much cover, but maybe they wouldn't need it for long. If they could make it to a farm road or highway, someone would possibly see them. Someone who didn't want to hit them with another stun gun and tie them up.

"Any idea who did this to us?" Seth asked. There it was again. The interrogating tone that made it sound as if she'd done something wrong.

"No." But Shelby immediately had to rethink her answer. "Wait. Maybe. There is this guy, Marvin Hance, who's mean enough and motivated enough to want to hurt me."

"The former FBI agent who was charged with killing his wife?" Seth didn't even hesitate.

"The very one. You know him?"

"Not personally, but I'm familiar with his case, and he still has friends in the FBI."

Hance did indeed, and Shelby had run up against a few of his friends who thought she was Satan himself to pursue their friend with her brand of journalism.

"Well, Hance isn't a friend of mine," she clarified. "I did some articles about him, and he didn't care much for them. Then the murder charges were dismissed on a technicality—"

"A botched search warrant," Seth supplied. "Hance has threatened you?"

"Oh, yes. Threats, phone calls, showing up at

my office. It got to the point where I had to get a restraining order."

The ordeal had been a nightmare. Well, not compared to this, but it'd been unpleasant. It also hadn't helped when some of Hance's FBI friends had made it next to impossible for her to get information about his murder investigation that would normally be provided to reporters.

Shelby shook her head. "I'm pretty sure Hance murdered his wife, and I believe he's capable of murdering again. But why would he possibly involve you in his mission to get back at me for those articles?"

Seth made a sound to indicate he was giving that some thought, and he walked around a rusted-out car. "The only thing that connects us is my mother's trial."

True. His stepbrother, Tucker, was married to her sister, Laine, but since Seth and his stepbrother were barely on speaking terms, that connection was thin.

But, for that matter, so was the trial.

"I believe Jewell's guilty," Shelby said, speaking out loud and hoping it made more sense than when it was still in her head. "You believe she's innocent. So if our captors or Hance did this because of the murder trial, what could they possibly hope to achieve?"

"I don't know why Hance would have involved

me in this. But someone else could have wanted to use us for some kind of ransom." He answered her question so quickly it was clear his head wasn't as foggy as hers. "But not ransom for money. Maybe someone wanted to use us to try to sway the trial in some way."

It didn't make sense, but neither did anything else about this situation. Shelby didn't have access to anything that could affect the trial.

Unlike Seth.

He probably could get at some evidence if necessary, but so far he didn't seem to be the law-breaking type. Maybe because he thought he had justice on his side and that Jewell would be cleared of all charges.

And that brought Shelby back to a revenge theory.

Maybe Hance wanted revenge against her and Seth had accidentally gotten caught up in the plan? It'd be a weird coincidence since both Seth and she had gotten phone calls that'd brought them here, but nothing else made sense right now.

Seth came to a stop so quickly that Shelby plowed into him. He was solid, all right, and didn't seem to notice she'd bumped into him. Instead, he just lifted his head.

"Get down," he said, but he didn't wait for her

to do that. Seth jerked her to the ground amid the weeds and grass.

Shelby heard it then. The car engine. Or rather the engine of a big truck.

Oh, God.

This had to be the men who'd kidnapped them.

She sucked in her breath. Held it, waiting and praying.

Once the men were inside the barn, maybe Seth and she could make a run for it to put some space between them and these killers. There weren't many places to hide, but she'd spotted some good-size boulders just ahead. That would give them far more protection and cover than the grass.

Shelby couldn't fully turn her head because of the way Seth was holding her, but from the corner of her eye she saw the driver park the truck. Two men got out. She didn't recognize either of them, but they were both armed with weapons not only in holsters but also in their hands. As she'd hoped, they went into the barn.

"Let's go," Seth mouthed.

He took her by the wrist and started running toward those boulders. She wasn't exactly a slouch at running, but Seth was a heck of a lot faster than she was. If he hadn't kept hold of her, she wouldn't have been able to keep up with him.

They were just a few yards away when Shelby heard something she didn't want to hear.

"There they are!" one of the men shouted.

Her heart went to her knees, and Seth dragged her back to the ground. Probably to stop them from being gunned down.

But the men didn't shoot.

There was another sound. The truck engine roared to life, and Seth's gaze snapped right in that direction.

"Run," Seth ordered, getting her to her feet again.

She did, but Shelby looked over her shoulder. And she heard the strangled sound claw its way through her throat.

The truck was no longer in front of the barn. Nor on the road.

It was coming right at them.

Chapter Three

Seth didn't look back. He just tightened his grip on Shelby's arm and kept running as fast as he could.

But the truck kept coming, too.

Just ahead were the boulders, and while they would have protected them from bullets, the truck would be able to drive around them and get to Shelby and him that way. Their best bet was to hide behind the small trees just ahead. The oaks were just large enough and close enough together that the driver should have trouble maneuvering around or through them.

Seth hoped so anyway.

The engine got louder. The truck, closer. So close he could practically feel the heat coming off the vehicle. And just when Seth thought the kidnappers would run them down, Shelby and he were able to duck behind the first tree. The driver slammed on his brakes but then darted into a small clearing to their left.

"He's trying to run us over," Shelby said, her breath gusting. "But why didn't he just shoot at us instead?"

Good question. Seth didn't have a good answer other than maybe the men still wanted them alive. They'd proved that by kidnapping rather than killing them at the warehouse. They were proving it now by not shooting at them. The problem was, Seth had no idea why someone wanted to put them through this.

Unless…

Maybe they wanted to set up Shelby and him to take the blame for that murder back at the warehouse.

Was that what this was all about?

If so that would explain why they'd both been lured to the warehouse with those calls. But it sure as heck didn't explain why Shelby and he had been targeted in the first place. Other than their connection to his mother and the upcoming trial, they didn't have anything in common.

Seth didn't have time to give it any more thought because the truck turned in the clearing and came straight for them again. He kept hold of Shelby in case she fell, and they raced behind another tree. Like before, the driver adjusted and started getting into a position where he could come after them again.

Shelby reached down, grabbed a huge rock

and hurled it at the truck. It smashed into the side window but didn't break the glass. She tossed another rock. So did Seth, though he figured it wouldn't stop the men. Still, it felt good to be inflicting some kind of damage.

The driver finally got the truck turned around and came toward them again. Shelby and he ran, ducking behind a small mesquite, and they hurled some more rocks. Seth sent one right into the windshield, and this time the safety glass cracked and webbed.

Good. Maybe it'd make it harder for the driver to see.

Or not.

Like before, the man threw the truck into Reverse and came right at them.

"We're running out of trees," Shelby said through the gusts of breath.

Yeah, they were, and that kicked up Seth's heartbeat even more. He looked around for anything they could use for cover or an escape.

He saw something.

About twenty yards away was a heap of dirt that appeared to be a natural embankment. Maybe to a small creek or stream. Since he didn't hear any water, Seth was hoping it was dry and too steep for the truck to go in.

"We're going there," he told Shelby, tipping his head to the embankment.

They raced to another tree, the final one, and Seth waited for the driver to throw the truck into Reverse before he started running. It didn't take long for the driver to adjust his course and aim the truck at them again.

Part of Seth wanted to stop, face their pursuers head-on and demand some answers. But that could be suicide. Just because these idiots hadn't fired shots at them so far didn't mean they wouldn't start now. Besides, he could demand answers once he caught them. And he *would* catch them. No way would he let them get away with this.

It seemed to take an eternity, but Shelby and he finally reached the embankment just a few seconds ahead of the truck. As Seth had hoped, it was a small creek bed, and it was plenty deep enough. At least five feet and dry.

Well, it was dry in this part of the bed anyway.

Just a short distance to his right some water pooled and the bed narrowed. To his left, the water was much shallower. And the truck would be able to get through there.

And it did.

The truck tore through the dirt embankment, dipped into the recessed area, but the huge tires got enough traction for the vehicle to make it to the other side.

Exactly where Seth had planned to go.

He'd already spotted a heavily treed area over there, but now he wouldn't be able to get to it.

Time for plan B.

"Let's go," he told Shelby.

And they started running along the creek bed where there was some mud and water. If the men wanted to come after them, then they'd have to get out of the truck and go on foot or else risk the truck bogging down.

It didn't take long for Shelby and him to reach the water. Thankfully, it was only ankle deep, but there was also soupy mud. Not the best running surface, especially since he was wearing cowboy boots and Shelby was in sandals. Still, they ran as if their lives depended on it because they very well could.

Even if this was some kind of kidnapping gone wrong, the men might want to cut their losses and just kill them. Shelby and he had to get out of their paths before that could happen.

"There they are," Seth heard one of the men yell.

Seth didn't stop running, but he glanced over his shoulder and spotted the two behind them in the creek bed.

Hell.

The men were now on foot and already too close. When they reached the water, it would slow them down as it had Shelby and him, but it wouldn't slow them down nearly enough. All the idiots needed to do was get in firing range. Even if they didn't have plans to kill them, they could still shoot Shelby and him to get them to stop.

"There's more water," Shelby warned him.

Yes, Seth saw it. Just ahead the bed not only widened, but the water got deeper. He figured that would only continue until they reached an honest-to-goodness creek.

"Are you a good swimmer?" Seth asked.

Shelby glanced at him. She was breathing through her mouth now, and her face was flushed from the exertion. "Not even close."

Well, there went plan C. He didn't want her to drown, and as exhausted as they already were, it'd likely take a strong swimmer for them to escape, especially if the men continued to follow them.

It was hard to think while running like a crazy man, but Seth forced himself to look around and see what their options were.

There weren't many.

They could keep running and hope the water didn't get so deep that it'd require swimming. But that was a huge gamble. Or he could stop and try to fight. If the men weren't armed, that was exactly what he would do, but those weapons gave them a huge advantage. Again, it was a gamble.

Seth thought of one other plan.

It was risky, too, but it might be the only chance they had.

He looked ahead, spotted a place that might work. The water was deeper there, but the embankment wasn't as high as in other places.

"When we stop," Seth told her, "I want you to start climbing up the embankment on your right."

"We're stopping?" she said on a gasp.

Panic was in her voice. In her eyes, too, and Seth hoped Shelby could hold it together long enough to do this. He'd been an FBI agent for nine years now. Plenty of time for him to be in situations with armed men. Still, he'd never been in a predicament like this.

In hindsight, he should have forced Shelby back into her car the moment she'd pulled up to the warehouse. He should have threatened her and made her go. If he'd done that, maybe she wouldn't be in this mess.

He'd kick himself for that later.

Later, after he saved her.

Seth tightened his grip on her arm, stopping her in her tracks, and he shoved her onto the embankment. Shelby dug in her heels and scrambled over. Seth did the same, and the second he was over the top, he grabbed her hand again and took off running. Not away from the men but rather in their direction.

Toward the truck.

The men cursed and tried to scramble up the embankment, too, but they chose a spot that was steep and muddy. Seth took full advantage of that and went into a sprint. Just behind him, Shelby kept up, and they made a beeline for the truck.

"Get them!" one of the men yelled.

Seth glanced back again. The men were no longer in the creek bed but were in the same clearing as he and Shelby. Both were still armed and running way too fast. Seth figured it wouldn't be long before they caught up with them.

The truck was just ahead, both the driver and passenger's doors wide-open. Seth didn't hear the engine running, but he hoped the guys had at least left the keys in the ignition. He knew how to hot-wire a car, but that took time. Time that Shelby and he didn't have.

"Get in and get down," Seth told her. This time she'd darn well better listen.

They scrambled toward the truck. Shelby toward the passenger's side and Seth behind the wheel. The keys were in there.

Thank God.

While the men ran straight toward them, Seth

started the engine and threw the vehicle into Reverse so he could turn around. Not easy to do with the trees and the embankment so close. It also didn't help that the broken front windshield looked more like a spider web.

"They're almost on us," Shelby said. She'd gotten on the floor as he'd ordered, but she lifted her head to peer out at the men.

Yes, they were that close. "Check for a weapon in the glove compartment or under the seat," he said.

That'd keep Shelby down and out of potential line of fire. And, besides, she might get lucky and actually find a gun or two.

Seth finally got the truck turned around and gunned the engine, but he didn't get very far before he had to slow down to swerve around more trees. Unfortunately, there was no direct path to the road so that meant he needed to turn around yet again and go back to the low spot in the embankment where the men had first crossed.

He hit the brakes and took the turn as fast as he could. The men were there, of course, coming right at them. And while he wanted answers, it'd be safer for Shelby and him if he just ran them down.

"No gun," Shelby said, rifling through the glove compartment. She was about to start her search under the seat, but she froze and her eyes widened. "You're driving right at them?"

"Hold on," Seth warned her, and he aimed the truck at the men.

They scattered, one going left and the other to the right, and they both hit the ground to get out of the way of the truck. Seth got a good look at them then. He didn't recognize either man, but he did recognize something—their concerned looks. Judging from the expressions, the duo had realized that he'd now seen their faces.

That meant he could possibly identify them.

In his experience, once you had the names of the criminals, then the motive would soon follow. Seth needed that because these two had almost certainly murdered that man back at the warehouse.

"There's no gun under the seat," Shelby relayed. She lifted her head again, this time looking out the back window. "And they're still running after us."

Seth glanced at the side mirror to see just how close they were. Too close. But he couldn't go any faster because he might hit a boulder or a tree. If that happened, Shelby and he would be sitting ducks.

Seth finally spotted the low embankment just ahead. A welcome sight. And a somewhat scary one if this plan didn't work.

"Hang on," he told Shelby.

She grabbed the door handle and the dashboard. Good thing, too. Because the impact tossed them around like rag dolls. Seth wasn't wearing a seat belt so his head hit the ceiling. Shelby's shoulder bashed against the door, causing her to make a sharp sound of pain.

But Seth didn't stop.

If he did, there was just enough soft ground that it might bog down the tires. So Seth slammed on the accelerator, and they got another hard jolt when he came up the other side. He headed for the driveway in front of the house and barn.

"Oh, God," Shelby said.

There was plenty of fear in her voice. Seth glanced in his rearview mirror and saw the reason for that brand new round of fear.

Both men had stopped and had taken aim.

Their guns were pointed right at the truck.

That barely had time to register in Seth's mind when he heard the blasts, and the back windshield came crashing down on Shelby and him.

"Cover your eyes and stay down," Seth ordered.

It wasn't a second too soon before more shots came, slicing through the glass and metal frame and sending a spray of shards right at them. He felt one of those slice his cheek, but he still didn't stop.

Didn't slow down.

With the bullets slamming into the truck, Seth sped to the driveway and then onto the dirt and gravel road.

Chapter Four

Shelby was in the enemy's camp, aka the Sweetwater Springs sheriff's office. She was plenty glad to be alive and away from those kidnappers, but this was the living, breathing definition of *uncomfortable*. Not just for her.

But for Seth, too.

Two of Jewell's sons were here: Sheriff Cooper McKinnon and his younger brother, Deputy Colt McKinnon. Both were on their phones. Both were working this investigation that'd just been dropped in their laps. Not only her and Seth's abduction, but also the murder of the man in the warehouse. Seth and she had already written out their statements, but Cooper had made it clear he still had more questions.

So did she, but she wasn't sure she'd find those answers here.

While Shelby wasn't on friendly terms with Cooper or Colt, the two brothers weren't exactly friendly with Jewell, either. In fact, judging from the frosty looks they were occasionally aiming at Seth, they also didn't care much for their step-brother. Probably because Jewell had raised Seth after abandoning them.

Yes, that definitely had created some tension.

Tension that had turned every muscle in Seth's body to iron. Not that Shelby had personal hands-on knowledge of that, because he'd kept his distance from her after they'd arrived at the sheriff's office. But she could tell from the grip Seth had on his borrowed phone and his terse responses to the caller that he was running on spent adrenaline and a steady dose of frustration.

Shelby knew exactly how he felt.

"Well?" she prompted the moment Seth finished his latest call. "Anything on the missing men who tried to kill us?"

He shook his head. "The FBI has a team looking for them. They'll turn up." Then Seth shot a narrowed glance at Cooper, who'd also just finished another round of calls. "Anything on that dead body?"

"I'm working on it," Cooper said, his voice practically a snarl. "The CSIs are processing both the barn and the warehouse now. Another is going through the kidnappers' truck that you drove here."

Shelby wondered if the local CSIs and FBI were actually cooperating with each other.

Maybe. Jurisdiction fell under the sheriff's office, but that clearly hadn't stopped Seth from calling in his FBI buddies. That might not sit well with Cooper. Of course, nothing probably sat well with him at the moment.

She didn't care who found answers. Shelby just wanted someone to get to the bottom of this.

Whatever *this* was.

"What about my truck and Shelby's car?" Seth asked. "Any sign of them?"

Cooper shook his head. "They weren't at the warehouse or the barn. No vehicles were found at either location."

Probably because the kidnappers hadn't wanted Seth and her to use them to attempt an escape. Still, if the vehicles turned up, they might contain clues as to who had moved them.

Seth didn't ask Cooper anything else. Or say anything to her. Instead, he launched into another call. Shelby wanted to make some calls of her own, but she didn't have a phone, and all the lines in the sheriff's office were tied up while they were still trying to track down those men.

Besides, the main reason she hadn't asked for a phone was because she really didn't have anyone to call.

Her brother Aiden was away on a trip with his fiancée and wouldn't be back until tomorrow. Her sister had her hands full taking care of her adopted twins. That left her mother, who was dealing with her own demons and had checked herself into a psychiatric facility. It would only make those demons worse to hear how close to dying her youngest daughter had come just a few hours earlier. Her mom would want to know the details. Details that Shelby didn't want to say aloud. The kidnapping. Being tied up.

Those gunshots.

She'd been through a lot of tense situations, but no one had ever fired shots at her and tried to murder her.

The sounds and images came flying at her like bullets. They hit her hard, causing her knees to buckle, and Shelby staggered a little before she could stop herself.

Seth was right there, even before the stagger ended, and he took hold of her arm and sat her down in the chair next to one of the deputy's desks. He didn't stop there. Though he didn't look particularly pleased about the chore, he went to the water cooler, filled a paper cup and brought it back to her.

"Drink this," he insisted. "And stay in that chair." No bedside manner. Zero. But the water was a nice touch since she actually might need it. Her throat felt ready to snap shut.

"I'm all right," she managed to say. "I'm just

a little dizzy." Along with the nerves zinging in her body.

Seth checked her eyes, no doubt trying to figure out if she was telling the truth or anything close to it. "When you got examined at the hospital, did the doctor say you'd get dizzy?" he asked.

Shelby nodded, sipped the water, stayed seated. "He said it was a possibility." Along with nausea and other unpleasant side effects. "They won't know what kind of drug was used on us until they get back lab results."

When Seth continued to stare at her, Shelby stopped in midsip and looked up. "Why? What did the doctor tell you?" Because it occurred to her then that Dr. Howland might have given her the diluted version of what she could expect. "Did those men do something to us that I should know about?"

Seth shook his head. "No. I'm not keeping anything from you."

Good. They were on the same information page. Well, hopefully.

At least there hadn't been a sexual assault. Shelby had been checked for that. For any signs of trauma, too, but other than scrapes, bruises and a single needle puncture mark on her arm, she was okay.

Physically anyway.

It might take forty years or so to stop hearing the sound of those gunshots. Or for her to forget what it felt like to be so close to dying.

"You're not dizzy," she pointed out.

Maybe because Seth didn't experience such lowly human reactions. He only shrugged and stared down at her with those icy blue eyes. They coordinated well with his icy expression.

Except that changed a little, too.

"Once we're done here, I'll drive you to your place so you can get some rest." Then Seth huffed, cursed under his breath and generally looked disgusted with himself for giving a flying fig about her well-being.

Shelby couldn't help herself. She smiled. A weak, temporary one, but a smile nonetheless.

Under different circumstances, she might have liked him. Would have definitely been attracted to him. A no-brainer since Seth had rockstar looks to go along with that toned body and tempting mouth.

But this wasn't different circumstances.

Something she always had to remind her body any time she was within breathing distance of the FBI cowboy.

The bothersome reminder of his hot looks probably had something to do with the fact that he'd saved her life multiple times during their escape. Shelby hated to owe him, but she did. If

Seth hadn't been with her in the warehouse and the woods, she likely wouldn't be sitting here in the enemy's camp. She'd be dead.

And speaking of the enemy, Cooper finished his latest call and strolled toward her.

"So tell me more about this anonymous call that you got earlier today," Cooper said to her. Like some of Seth's earlier questions, it sounded like an accusation.

Shelby ignored the tone, the hard look and tried to give the sheriff something, *anything*, that would help with this investigation. "The caller was a man, and he said there was evidence about Jewell's trial in the warehouse."

That earned her a skeptical look from both Colt and Cooper.

"If I had my phone, I could show you the number," Shelby added. "But since the kidnappers took it, the only other thing I can tell you is that I didn't recognize his voice. He had no distinguishable accent and didn't give away any details about his identity or location."

The skeptical looks turned flat, and Seth even joined in on it.

"An anonymous caller tells you to go to an abandoned warehouse in the middle of nowhere, and you don't think that's suspicious?" Cooper pressed.

"Not really. I'm an investigative reporter. I get calls like that all the time."

Okay, that was a white lie. But she did occasionally get them, and she almost always followed through on them. She'd rethink that for future calls, though.

Shelby huffed. "Look, any time anyone contacts me and says they have information about my father's murder, I check it out. Period."

She owed him that, even though no one in this room was on board with this particular crusade. Not even her own siblings. And especially not the other residents of Sweetwater Springs. Her father hadn't been well liked because of his womanizing and cutthroat business dealings. That didn't matter to Shelby, though. He was her dad, and she'd make sure Jewell paid for killing him.

Cooper stared at her. A long time. So long that Seth stepped in front of her. "Someone set Shelby and me up. We need to find out who and why."

Seth and the sheriff were almost the same height and weight. They had similar glares that they traded when their gazes connected.

"So who would have set you up?" Cooper asked.

Seth tapped his badge. "Anybody who wanted to get back at me because of this." Then he paused. "But no one that I can think of who's connected to both Shelby and me. And trust me, I've been trying to come up with someone who'd fit that bill."

When Cooper's attention came back to her, Shelby knew it was her turn to answer. "I have a restraining order against Marvin Hance, the guy who got away with murder."

She saw the instant recognition in Cooper's eyes. Hance had certainly gotten a lot of press before and after his arrest. Thanks to her.

"Hance hates me because of the articles I wrote about him," Shelby continued. "And other than his friends still in the FBI, he hates people with badges because he thinks they should have done more to clear his name. Maybe Hance figured that he wanted to set me up for murder and snare a cop or an FBI agent in the process."

Except something about that theory didn't make sense, and the sound Seth made let her know he was thinking the same thing. If this was a setup, then why had those men kidnapped Seth and her and taken them to that barn? It would have been a better setup to leave them in the warehouse. A lot less work, too.

"I'll get Hance in here for questioning," Cooper insisted, and he took out his phone, no doubt to do that, but the sound of Colt's voice stopped him.

"We got an ID on the dead body from the warehouse. Randy Boutwell," Colt announced when he finished his call. Like Cooper, the deputy came closer to them.

Shelby repeated the name several times and shook her head. "Never heard of him."

Seth had a similar response. "Who is he?"

"An unemployed bartender from San Antonio," Colt answered, reading from his notes. "Fifty-six years old. He has an old record for shoplifting and petty theft."

Not exactly a hardened criminal, but maybe their paths had crossed at some point. She had to deal with all sorts of unsavory people sometimes to do research for her articles.

"San Antonio PD is running a background on him now," Colt added.

Good. Something might turn up as to why someone would want him dead. Someone who could explain all of this.

"What about the mask that was on Boutwell?" Shelby asked.

Mercy, her voice actually cracked. It was silly to hate a sign of weakness such as that, but she did. Especially in front of these cowboy cops.

The three lawmen exchanged glances, and it was Colt who finally shrugged. "Nothing on it. The CSIs will process it for prints and trace."

Which meant if the killer had half a brain there likely wouldn't be any evidence left behind.

"The mask is a blown-up shot of the photo that the newspapers ran after my father was murdered," she told them.

"After Whitt's blood was found in the cabin," Seth corrected.

Technically, Seth was right. There'd been blood, plenty of it, in the hunting cabin where her father and Jewell had met for their romantic trysts.

But no body.

At first the cops had ruled her dad a missing person, and that was when the particular photo had been splattered in the newspapers. He'd stayed listed as a missing person for more than twenty years until Shelby had pressured the new DA to reprocess the evidence. When Jewell's DNA had been discovered on the bloody sheets, the woman finally had been arrested. And when Whitt's bone fragments had been found a few months earlier, it had looked like a slam dunk case for the prosecution.

Still did.

"Was that why Randy Boutwell was killed?" Though Shelby hadn't intended to say it aloud. She also hadn't expected the trio of lawmen to know what she meant, but the scowl Seth gave her said otherwise.

"No," Seth snapped. "Nobody in my family killed Boutwell to make my mother look innocent."

"But it's an interesting theory," Shelby said. "Jewell's in jail. No way could she have killed Boutwell herself, but this might put reasonable doubt in the jurors' minds that my father's killer is still out there."

Oh, that didn't sit well with any of them.

Not that she had expected it would.

Cooper and Colt certainly wouldn't have done something like this. Or at least she hadn't thought they would since they were essentially estranged from Jewell, but Jewell had kids who loved her. Her twin daughters, Rosalie and Rayanne.

And her stepson, Seth, of course.

Seth looked her straight in the eyes. "Your father's killer *is* still out there."

Shelby didn't dodge that stare. "Then, we'll have to agree to disagree about that."

They could add it to the other mountain of things they disagreed about. Except Shelby immediately rethought that. The only thing they actually disagreed about was Jewell. Obviously, though, that was enough of a six-hundred-pound gorilla.

Cooper volleyed glances between Seth and her and finally gave a low groan. "You're both free to go, but don't leave town. I might have other questions for you."

That order didn't sit well with Seth. It got his jaw tight again. Of course, anything Cooper could have said might have caused that reaction.

"I'll be at my house," Shelby mumbled. "Seth will probably be at the McKinnon ranch, where you and your brothers can personally keep an eye on him."

Literally.

Since Seth had been living in the guesthouse for months, waiting on his mother's trial, and the guesthouse was a stone's throw from both Colt's and Cooper's houses.

Shelby started toward the door, but when Seth didn't budge, she stopped and looked back at him. "Still planning to give me a ride to my house?"

Seth exchanged a few glances with the McKinnons and then added some profanity. "I'll wait at her place with her," he growled to Cooper. "Just find these kidnappers fast. And I'll need a gun and a phone until the FBI can bring me replacements."

Maybe it was her frazzled nerves, but it took Shelby a few seconds for that to sink in. It didn't sink in well.

"You think you're staying with me?" she

asked. "Because we both know that's not a good idea."

Seth gave her a flat look and took the gun and cell phone that Colt handed him. "Those two men might come after you again. You really want to be alone when that happens, huh?"

She opened her mouth to say yes, that she wanted to be alone so she could get her head on straight, but the *yes* lodged in her throat. Shelby didn't want to have to fend off those men again. She probably couldn't win.

But then, it might be just as dangerous to be under the same roof with Seth.

Seth put the gun in his shoulder holster, slipped the phone into his pocket. "If the sheriff hasn't found those men by morning," he added, "I'll get you a safe house."

Shelby didn't want that, either. Didn't want to be tucked away so that she couldn't get to the bottom of what was happening. She had to come up with an alternative plan, one that didn't involve Seth or the McKinnons.

But what?

She didn't even get a chance to give that some thought because Cooper's phone rang, and he stepped away to take the call. Maybe, just maybe, this was news that the kidnappers had been caught. While she was hoping, maybe the person who'd killed Boutwell had been caught, as well. If so, then she could go home and not have to be afraid of her own shadow.

However, one glance at Cooper's face and Shelby knew she hadn't gotten that lucky.

"Send me the picture," Cooper said to whoever was on the other end of the line. Several moments later his phone made a dinging sound.

"What's wrong?" she asked the moment Cooper finished the call. His attention stayed on the phone screen for what seemed an eternity.

The sheriff didn't jump to answer. Nor did he aim another hard look at her. This time when Cooper looked at her, she saw something else in his eyes. Concern maybe?

No.

It was sympathy.

Oh, no. This was going to be bad.

"The CSIs out at the warehouse found another body," Cooper finally said.

Yes, bad, all right.

Mercy. Her knees nearly buckled again, and Shelby slapped her hand on the wall to stop herself from falling. The shock of hearing there was another body was enough to send her stomach into a tailspin, but Cooper had no doubt encountered other dead bodies.

Ones that hadn't put that look of sympathy on his face.

"Oh, God," Shelby managed to say. "Is it someone I know?"

"Maybe." Cooper held up the phone so she could see the image on the screen. Seth came closer so he could have a look.

At first Shelby couldn't figure out what she was seeing exactly.

"The dead woman was wearing a picture mask," Cooper explained. "Like the one on the man in the warehouse."

Shelby swallowed hard. Except the man had a mask of her father. This time, it was Shelby's face on the screen. A photo that was often printed along with her articles.

Beneath the mask the woman had a piece of white paper clutched in her lifeless hands. And Shelby had no trouble seeing what was typed there.

"You're a traitor, Shelby Braddock. And soon you'll be a dead one."

Chapter Five

Traitor.

That one word kept repeating through Seth's mind. Not that the other words in the threatening note hadn't been powerful enough. After all, the person who'd written it likely had committed two murders and had planned to do the same to Shelby.

The note wasn't especially different from other death threats he'd read. Death threats that he'd gotten as an FBI agent.

Except for *traitor.*

He'd been called plenty of things, but traitor wasn't one of them. So what had Shelby done to get that label slapped on her? And who'd done the labeling by writing that note?

So far Shelby hadn't volunteered anything, even when Seth had asked her point-blank. She'd just sat quietly in the truck that he'd borrowed from Cooper and kept watch as Seth had driven them to her house.

Something that he'd been doing, too.

He didn't want those two men coming out of the woodwork to follow them. So far, though, they'd had the road leading out of town to themselves. If Seth had been alone, he would have welcomed coming face-to-face with those idiots. This time, though, he had a gun and could do something about getting answers as to who had hired them.

And why.

But as long as Shelby was with him, he preferred to postpone the confrontation. Maybe he wouldn't have to wait too long to dole out some justice. Ditto for not waiting too long for other arrangements for Shelby's safety. For now, though, he was her best bet at staying alive, though he figured she wouldn't want to admit that.

He'd never been to Shelby's place so he followed her nonchatty directions of "turn here" and "about a mile up on the right" coupled with some gestures and pointing. It wasn't that far from town, only about ten minutes from the sheriff's office, but it definitely qualified as rural. And it certainly wasn't the palace he'd been expecting—considering Shelby's family was filthy rich.

Seth pulled the truck to a stop in front of the modest one-story wood-frame house. White with dark green shutters and door. It sat in the middle of pastureland that even included a rundown barn and corral. No animals, though, except for a pair of cats sleeping on the porch. When Seth got out they skittered toward the barn.

"It was my aunt's house," Shelby explained, probably because Seth was looking a little gob smacked. "She left it to me when she died."

"You didn't want to live in the big house with your mother?" he asked. Seth had never been inside that place, either, but he'd seen it from a distance, and it probably had twenty or more rooms.

"I can only take my mother in small doses," she said almost in a whisper.

She retrieved a key from a nearby terra-cotta pot with a dead plant and used it to open the door. He was surprised again when he heard the warning beeps of a security system, and Shelby entered a code into what appeared to be a brand-new keypad next to the door and disarmed it.

"Marvin Hance," she explained. "After he started threatening me, I had a security system installed."

Good. That was a start. Seth drew his gun and stepped in ahead of her. Until that moment she probably hadn't considered that someone could get past a security system and be hiding.

Such as kidnappers.

"Wait here," he warned Shelby.

She stayed put while Seth went from room to room. Only five of them. A living room, kitchen and two bedrooms and a bath off the hall.

Shelby wasn't the neatest housekeeper. The desk in the corner of the living room was piled high with files and photos. Dishes were in the kitchen sink. And on the bathroom floor lay a bra and panties.

Devil red.

Seth wasn't sure why that hooked his attention, but it did. Probably because he could imagine how those devilish-colored underthings would look on Shelby's body.

Something that he wished hadn't crossed his mind.

It kept crossing his mind after he finished his search and went back to the front door to shut and lock it.

"Is something wrong?" Shelby asked, studying his expression.

Yeah. But he'd take it to the grave. No way Seth would admit that her underwear had reminded him of this blasted unwanted attraction he felt for her.

Seth holstered his gun and used the borrowed phone to fire off a text to a fellow agent, Austin Duran, giving him the address of Shelby's house and requesting a new gun, vehicle, a change of clothes and a phone. It'd take Austin a while to get all that together, but at least Austin was in the area. In fact, he lived on the grounds of the McKinnon ranch with his wife, Rosalie.

Jewell's daughter and Seth's stepsister.

Since Seth had been raised with Rosalie and her twin, Rayanne, they were as close as siblings could be. He loved them both, but it would put a strain on their relationship once his sisters learned he was protecting Shelby.

Ditto for this whole lust thing going on.

As if she knew what he was thinking, Shelby looked at him. Shook her head. "This is as uncomfortable for me as it is for you."

She rubbed her forehead, glanced around before her gaze landed on his chest. That was when Seth realized his shirt was halfway open, the buttons likely lost during the kidnapping or that chase through the woods. She reached out as if to fix it, but Shelby quickly snatched back her hand.

"Sorry," she said. "That kind of stuff could get me labeled as a traitor by certain members of my family and yours."

"Traitor," Seth repeated. "Interesting choice of words." Now he shook his head. "I don't want to go another round with you blaming someone in my family for what happened to us."

"No," she agreed. She headed toward that

cluttered desk. "But I think I might have some idea about the traitor comment."

As she pushed aside some papers and turned on her computer, something else caught Seth's eye. The printed-out charts and papers that she'd taped to the wall above her desk. It was a timeline with notes that dated back twenty-three years to the day her father had gone missing.

Even though the details were all etched in his mind, Seth went through them. Step by painful step. The blood found in Whitt Braddock's cabin. The cabin where he'd supposedly met Jewell for their affair. An affair that'd ended when Whitt had broken off things and told her he was reconciling with his wife.

That was the motive the prosecution would use to try to convict Jewell.

The DA would try to paint her as a woman scorned, and the theory would be bolstered by the fact that just two days after Whitt's disappearance, Jewell had gathered up her young twin daughters and left Sweetwater Ranch to move several counties away.

Jewell's leaving had worked out well for Seth since Jewell and her husband, Roy, had divorced, and a few years later, Jewell had married Seth's father. Seth had been twelve. She'd been the mother Seth had never had since his had died when he was just a toddler.

His attention went back to the charts, to the years Shelby had tried to get the cops and DA to reopen her father's missing person's case. She'd finally accomplished that almost a year ago. Items taken from the cabin had been tested, and Jewell's DNA had been found on the bloody sheets. Whitt's blood mixed with her DNA wasn't a good sign.

Nine months ago, Jewell had been arrested.

That was on the chart, too.

Then the bone fragments had been found three months ago, and once they'd been positively identified as Whitt's, Shelby had dug in even harder to get Jewell convicted. Seth had done the same thing to get his mother's name cleared. Especially since he hadn't liked the timing of those recovered fragments.

"Don't you think it's suspicious that it took twenty-three years to find those bone pieces?" Seth asked.

She looked up at him. Frowned. "What are you saying?"

"I thought I was pretty clear. It's suspicious. Cops, PIs and CSIs combed over every inch of the cabin and the grounds, and those fragments didn't surface until just a few months before my mother's trial."

"They're fragments," she pointed out. "Easy to miss."

But she didn't sound so certain of that. Probably because Shelby herself had thoroughly searched the grounds. Seth certainly had.

"You're thinking my father's *real* killer could have hidden his body all this time and then planted the fragments?" she suggested. "There's not an ounce of proof for that."

No, there wasn't, but that didn't mean it hadn't happened.

"Now, back to the whole traitor thing," she continued a moment later after she huffed.

Shelby scrolled through some internet links and opened one. It was a blog on a site called Justice Hunters. Seth hadn't read this specific one, but he was familiar with sites such as this dedicated to solving cold cases.

"The person who runs the blog is a friend of mine, and I occasionally do posts for her," Shelby explained.

That in itself wasn't surprising because of Shelby's job, but what was a surprise was the title of the blog, "A New Look at My Father's Murder."

"Don't read a lot into this," she went on. "My friend had asked if I'd explored all angles of this case, and this tells everyone that I did."

Seth leaned in for a closer look. Yes, this was definitely a new look at the investigation, since it mentioned some of Seth's big concerns.

Concern number one: just because Jewell's

DNA was on the sheets, it didn't mean she'd killed Whitt.

"Your dad was a big man," Seth agreed. "And it would have taken two people to move the body. Jewell's husband, Roy, has an alibi, so we know it wasn't him. But Jewell wasn't Whitt's only alleged lover."

She huffed again and pointed to their names in the blog. "Annette Prior and Meredith Bellows. I've interviewed them multiple times over the years, and both said they're innocent."

"Lots of guilty people say that. Both were married at the time of the affairs, so they had motive to try to conceal the fact that they'd been in that cabin with Whitt. Also, if Whitt had broken things off with them as well, either of them could be the killer. Or maybe both."

Shelby didn't exactly jump to argue with him about that.

And that was concern number two. Meredith had a thin alibi for the time of the murder, claiming she'd been recovering from a root canal and was home in bed and heavily sedated. Her dentist had verified that, but people still could kill under the right kind of sedation.

However, Annette's alibi was worse than thin. She, too, claimed to be at home all day, alone. And her car had never left the driveway. But she could have used another vehicle to get out to the cabin. One that she'd taken from her garage, and she could have driven the back roads to get from her house to the cabin.

Which brought him to concern number three.

"These are just the two women that we know about," he said. "Your father wasn't exactly a saint when it came to keeping his jeans zipped."

"I acknowledge all of that in the blog," Shelby admitted, her tone frostier than usual. "But neither Meredith nor Annette's DNA was found in the cabin."

Seth lifted his shoulder. "Then, why do the blog?"

"Because I wanted everyone to know that I was still after the truth. If there was any truth left to be discovered, that is."

Hell. And that was what *traitor* was all about. "You rattled somebody's cage. The killer's cage," Seth corrected.

Shelby practically leaped to her feet. "Don't go there. It was just a *what if* kind of post." She stopped, squeezed her eyes shut a moment. "But someone could have taken it the wrong way. Someone who cared for my father and wants Jewell convicted."

Or someone who didn't want to face murder charges.

Seth took out his phone. "I want Annette and Meredith brought back in for questioning."

However, Seth didn't even get a chance to text Austin again because he heard the sound of an approaching car. He shoved his phone back into his pocket and drew his gun while he hurried to the window. Maybe this was Austin arriving with the things Seth needed.

But no such luck.

It definitely wasn't Austin who stepped from the black two-door car that came to a stop in front of the house. But it was someone Seth instantly recognized.

What the hell was *he* doing here?

ONE LOOK AT their visitor and Shelby could have sworn her heart dropped to her knees.

It was Marvin Hance.

She wanted to be brave and not feel that punch of fear at just seeing his face. But she failed.

Shelby felt the fear, all right. She remembered every one of his threats. All the run-ins with him. Each of the times he'd made her feel as if he could crush her skull for speaking the truth about him getting off scot-free for murdering his wife.

"Did you know he was coming?" Seth asked her.

"No." Shelby couldn't say that fast enough. "I still have a restraining order on him."

Cursing, Seth handed her his borrowed phone.

"Call Cooper and tell him we have a situation. I want him out here to arrest Hance. I'd do it myself, but this could be a trap to lure us out so the kidnappers can get to us."

Good grief. She hadn't even thought of that, which caused Shelby to silently curse. She couldn't let the fear cloud her thoughts when dealing with a dangerous man such as Hance, because he could indeed be the one who'd hired those kidnappers. That gave her the burst of anger and focus she needed.

"Shelby?" Hance called out. "We have to talk."

"Disarm the security system," Seth ordered her.

She did, but she caught on to Seth's arm when he went for the door. "Remember, this could be a trap to get us outside."

"I'm not going outside. I'm just having a word with this idiot. Now call Cooper and tell him what I said."

Shelby did, and she kept the conversation with the sheriff short since she wanted to hear what Hance was going to say about this visit.

"Special Agent Calder," Hance greeted when Seth opened the door. He said Seth's name as if it was some kind of disease. "I heard about the kidnapping and figured you'd be here."

"Why are you here?" Seth demanded. "Shelby has a restraining order against you."

"Don't worry. I'll only be a second. I know Shelby's scared spitless of me, but I just want to talk to her."

That riled her to the core. She hated that this piece of slime could push her buttons, and even though she knew Seth wouldn't like it, Shelby stepped into the doorway beside him. She wanted to let Hance see that the fear card wasn't going to work. She aimed her hardest glare at him.

Hance didn't glare back. The corner of his mouth hitched into a smile that many people would have believed was genuine. A wolf in sheep's clothing. Hance looked like a TV evangelist with his styled-to-a-T bronze hair, angelic expression and pricey gray suit.

Shelby knew he was in his early forties, but he looked much younger. And he was strong. Beneath that suit was a muscled, violent man with a fierce grip. A former FBI agent who'd been trained to fight. Shelby had firsthand knowledge of just how strong that grip could be and just how vicious his words and threats were.

"We have nothing to talk about," she assured Hance. "But I know Sheriff McKinnon wants to talk to you."

"Yes, about the attack on you and Agent Calder." He glanced at the road behind him. "I figure he'll be here soon."

Neither Shelby nor Seth verified that, but as a former agent, Hance would know it was standard procedure to call for backup. And that he would be arrested for violating that restraining order.

"What do you want?" Seth repeated.

"Well, I'm not here about those scathing articles that Shelby wrote about me, even though my lawyers will soon have responses to those."

More threats. Hance was always claiming he was going to file a lawsuit against her for libel, but so far he hadn't. Probably because he didn't want to go another round with the legal system. He'd gotten lucky last time, but his luck might not continue to hold.

Hance stared at her, no doubt watching to see if the threat bothered her. It did. But only because he was delivering it personally. However, Shelby made sure he didn't see any discomfort in her expression or body language.

Unlike Seth's body language.

No discomfort, but he kept shooting her narrowed-eyed looks, probably silent warnings for her to go back inside.

She stayed put.

"Earlier today I got a call," Hance finally continued. "The person said I should go to the abandoned warehouse on Miller Road, that there'd be evidence I could use in the lawsuits I plan to file against Shelby."

An anonymous call like the ones Seth and she had gotten. Of course, Hance could be lying about getting such a call because he had arranged the ones to Seth and her.

"You have proof of this call?" Seth asked.

Hance nodded. "The number's on my phone. I'll turn it over to the sheriff once he gets here."

"That's not proof," Shelby fired back. "You could have hired someone to call you."

"True," Hance readily admitted, adding another of those damnable smiles. "But the only reason I'd do something like that would be to cover up that I was the one who orchestrated the attack against you. I didn't," he added calmly.

"You got proof of that?" Seth asked again.

No smile this time. Obviously, this was a conversation Hance would have preferred to have without the armed FBI agent who was giving him another cold, hard stare.

"Hard to prove something like that," Hance answered. "But I wanted Shelby to know that I didn't set this up. Just the opposite. It's obvious someone tried to set me up to take the fall for this."

"And why would someone do that?" she asked.

Hance lifted his shoulders. "I have motive because of the bad blood between us. But ask yourself this." He tipped his head to Seth without taking his attention off her. "If I'd wanted to get back at you, then why would I have involved him in this?"

Shelby wanted to believe there was a reason, but she couldn't readily think of one. The masks didn't help, either, because this didn't seem connected to Hance but rather her father's murder. And Hance didn't have any links to that. He had been just a teenager when Jewell had killed Whitt.

"I'm not sure what's going on with you and Agent Calder," Hance continued, aiming his words at her. "But keep me out of it. I don't want to be in the middle of whatever games you're playing to have Agent Calder's mother convicted."

Shelby huffed. "You think I'm responsible for that anonymous call you supposedly got? Well, I'm not."

"I don't care," Hance snapped. "Just don't involve me or you'll find yourself slapped with a restraining order of your own."

He'd hardly finished that idiotic threat when Shelby heard the siren. It didn't take long for the Sweetwater Springs cruiser to pull to a stop in front of her house. Colt stepped out.

"Marvin Hance?" Colt asked, already taking out handcuffs.

Hance nodded and extended his hands in surrender. "My lawyers are already on the way to the sheriff's office," he said to no one in particular. "While there, they'll file a complaint against Shelby and then begin a lawsuit against your department to stop this harassment."

Colt ignored all of that, cuffed him and led Hance to the rear seat of the cruiser. He locked the door but didn't get in with Hance. Instead, Colt walked toward Seth and her. At first Shelby thought it was for a tongue-lashing about all the trouble she was causing the McKinnons. But his expression said otherwise.

"We got an ID on the dead woman wearing the mask of your face," Colt said. "Her name's Claudia Ford. Like Boutwell, she had a record for petty stuff. Any chance you knew her?"

Shelby shook her head. Seth did, too, several moments later. "Does she have a connection to Boutwell?" Seth asked.

"None that immediately popped up, but we did get something else on Boutwell." Colt paused and then took a sheet of paper from his pocket and unfolded it before showing it to them.

It was a copy of a bank statement.

Boutwell wasn't exactly a rich man. The money seemed to go out as quickly as it came in to the account, and the deposits were well under five hundred dollars.

Except for one.

It was for three grand. A small fortune for a man like Boutwell.

"Notice the date," Colt instructed.

Seth took the bank statement, and together Shelby and he had a closer look. It didn't take long for her to see the date of the deposit.

And to know what it meant.

Or possibly could mean.

"My father's bone fragments," she managed to say around the sudden lump in her throat. "That's the date the fragments were found." Shelby immediately shook her head. "This doesn't mean anything."

She hoped.

"There's more," Colt said, taking out another piece of paper. "Boutwell got a speeding ticket that same day. Deputy Pete Nichols was the one who pulled him over."

"Nichols," Seth repeated. Colt nodded. "Boutwell was in Sweetwater Springs the morning the bone fragments were discovered. And Pete pulled him over less than a mile from the Braddock cabin where Whitt was supposedly murdered."

Shelby felt as if someone had slugged her in the stomach.

If Boutwell had indeed been paid to put those bones near the cabin, then who had hired him to plant evidence that would ensure Jewell's conviction for murder? And how had that person gotten the bones in the first place?

Only one answer came to mind.

A bad one.

Sweet heaven, was her father's killer really still out there?

Chapter Six

This was *not* how Seth had intended to spend the night and following morning.

He'd planned on using the time to go over the latest developments in the investigation. Alone. At his office or back at the guesthouse at the McKinnon ranch, where he'd been staying for the past seven months. He certainly hadn't planned on being under the same roof with Shelby.

Yet, here he was.

Drinking his third cup of coffee at her kitchen table, watching the sunrise and waiting for Shelby to wake up so he could give her yet another dose of bad news.

As if she hadn't already had enough.

The news about the money deposited into Boutwell's account had shaken her up. No doubt because she now had to face the truth.

That Jewell possibly hadn't killed her father after all.

And that the person who had killed him had planted those bone fragments for someone to find.

Of course, Shelby wouldn't accept it as fact just on the basis of the three grand someone had given the man. She'd need a lot more than that. Ditto for the DA, and with Seth's stepmother's trial now just two days away, they were running out of time to find something to prove to everyone that Jewell was innocent.

And she was innocent.

However, Seth hated that voice in the back of his head that whispered, *What if she isn't?*

His mother didn't have a violent bone in her body, but maybe she'd been pushed to the limit. Seth hated to admit that, too. Hated that he was starting to have any doubts about her.

Yeah, it was definitely time to put some distance between Shelby and him.

He finally heard Shelby stirring in her bedroom. Several minutes later, she turned on the shower. Seth glanced at his phone again, willing it to ring with good news that would put an end to this.

Nothing.

But at least it was his own phone and not a borrowed one from Cooper. Seth could thank his brother-in-law for that. Austin had brought Seth not only the phone but also his laptop, a weapon and a change of clothes. Along with playing deliveryman, Austin had even offered to pull night duty guarding Shelby.

Something Seth had strongly considered.

But Austin and Seth's sister Rosalie had a toddler daughter, and with Rosalie on edge because of Jewell's approaching trial, Seth figured Austin already had his hands full.

He heard Shelby turn off the shower and tried to brace himself for all the bad news he had to tell her. However, he heard a sound that pushed all that bad news to the back burner.

Shelby gasped, followed by a strangled sound that Seth had no trouble interpreting.

Fear.

That got him to his feet. Seth slapped down his coffee cup and ran toward the bathroom. Since Shelby's room was the first one in the hall, he got there in a matter of seconds and drew his gun along the way.

Seth didn't knock and wasn't sure what he'd find when he threw open the door, but what he saw was a half-naked Shelby standing at her bedroom window. A flimsy white robe clung to her still-damp body. She whirled around, her hands coming up as if expecting a fight, and her breath swooshed out when she saw him.

"Outside," she managed to say.

He went closer, automatically pushing her

away from the window and behind him, and looked out into the yard.

Hell.

There, on the grass outside her window, someone had spray painted a single word in bright yellow paint.

Traitor.

"Those men were here," she said, her voice strangled. "Less than five feet from my bedroom window."

Yes. If not the kidnappers, then someone working for the same scumbag who'd hired them.

Seth glanced around the yard, looking for any signs of who'd done this, but he didn't see anyone. It also didn't appear to be fresh paint. Bits of leaves covered some of the letters.

"Did you look out the window last night?" he asked her.

She shook her head, and because she was wobbly again, Seth hooked his arm around her waist, had her sit on the bed and closed the curtains.

"Wait here," he insisted before hurrying through the rest of the house to look out each window.

No one was out there, thank God.

"Someone could have painted that while we were at the sheriff's office yesterday," Seth reminded Shelby when he went back into her bedroom. "Or even earlier."

He'd checked the house when they'd arrived, but he certainly hadn't looked at that area of the yard other than to look for any signs of a gunman. It was a reminder that he needed to move Shelby to a safer place. One where idiots couldn't get this close to her.

"This person wants me scared," she whispered. "They're succeeding. I'm scared."

Seth figured it took a lot for her to admit that. He wasn't usually a fan of giving in to fear, but in this case, it served a purpose. It could make Shelby more cautious. More agreeable to a plan that she wasn't going to like much.

"I want you to go somewhere," he said. "Somewhere other than here, where you'll be safe."

Despite her admission of fear, she still shook her head, just as Seth figured she would. "But once the men who kidnapped us are found—"

"They're still at large." That was the first round of bad news. He dragged in a deep breath before he continued with things she definitely wasn't going to want to hear. "Hance is already out on bail. He'll be charged with violating the restraining order, but he probably won't get any jail time for it."

Shelby stayed quiet a moment. Processing. "I see."

Since the string of bad news would only strengthen his argument for her to leave and go to a safe house, Seth continued, "Cooper brought in both Meredith and Annette for questioning last night. Both claimed they were innocent. Both even agreed to let Cooper examine their bank records so they could prove that they haven't paid out money for hired guns and kidnappers."

Seth could dismiss the women's claims of innocence, but according to Cooper, they'd both fully cooperated. Both had even provided alibis for the time Shelby and he had been kidnapped. Of course, it'd been hired goons who'd done that, but he still didn't have any proof to warrant arresting Meredith or Annette.

Shelby sat there, clearly trying to steel herself. It didn't appear to be working. This next bit of news wouldn't help with that.

"The FBI looked through phone records to determine who made that anonymous call to you, the one that lured you to the warehouse. It was made from a burner cell. No way to trace it, and it was the same number used to call Hance."

"Hance could have made the call to himself," she pointed out quickly.

Seth nodded. Hard to rule that out.

She stared at him. "There's more?"

"Yeah." And this time Seth eased down on the foot of the bed so they'd be eye to eye. "The CSIs finished processing the barn where we were tied up. They found more rope, a butcher knife and paper masks. This time of you and me."

"Oh, God." She pressed her fingers to her mouth for a moment and then repeated it.

That'd been his reaction, too. Yes, he'd figured someone wanted to do them bodily harm, but those masks, knife and ropes meant someone had planned to kill them there and stage the bodies as the others had been.

If Seth went with the most obvious theory, that meant someone had tried to get Shelby, Hance and him to the warehouse. Together. Maybe so Hance could be set up to take the fall for murdering them. Or maybe Hance had hoped for some reverse psychology to make himself look innocent.

"Do you have any good news whatsoever?" she asked.

He had to give that some thought. "We're alive."

A burst of air left her mouth. Almost a laugh, but there was no humor in it. She stood as if ready to bolt, but Seth took hold of her arm to stop her.

Not the best idea he'd ever had.

Because she whirled around, his grip on her

wrist stopping her, but it sent her colliding right into him. They'd had some experience dodging each other, but this time Shelby didn't *dodge*. She stayed put, melting against Seth while she slid her arm around him.

She smelled good, like shampoo, soap and mint toothpaste. He'd never considered those scents to be major turn-ons, but like her underwear, they seemed to be now.

"Don't tell me this is dangerous," she argued. "Everything about us right now is dangerous."

He couldn't argue with that. They'd had enough bad news to last a couple lifetimes, and whether he wanted it or not, it felt good to have Shelby in his arms.

And it felt bad, too.

Very, very bad.

That should have been enough for Seth to step back. Especially when Shelby stared up at him. No tears in her pale gray eyes. Just that worried look followed by a different kind of look that he'd come to recognize.

Oh, man. Not this.

Not with her wearing only that skimpy robe and smelling fresh from the shower.

Seth was cursing that look, but he should have been cursing himself. Because he was the one who made things a thousand times worse by taking his grip off her wrist and moving his hand to the back of her neck. Dragging her closer. Until he lowered his head and put his mouth to hers.

Now he had a different reason to curse himself. Because with just a touch the fire came. Not a little spark, either. This was a full blast of heat that he darn sure didn't want. Not with Shelby anyway.

Did that stop him?

No, and it sure as heck didn't stop her.

Shelby did her own share of gripping. Pulling him closer. And deepening the kiss. As if it needed any deepening. It already felt like scalding-hot foreplay and perhaps would have turned into just that.

If his phone hadn't rang.

Seth welcomed the sound as much as he welcomed the long breath that he pulled into his air-starved lungs. However, that welcome feeling didn't last long when he saw Cooper's name on the screen.

"I need good news," Seth snapped when he answered. News that would put an end to these close quarters with Shelby.

"I'm sorry," Cooper said, sounding genuine. And upset. "But there's been another murder. This time it's someone Shelby knows."

SHELBY SPOTTED THE crime scene tape the moment Seth took the turn onto the dirt road that led to her father's hunting cabin. The very place he'd been murdered twenty-three years ago.

Now, according to Cooper, another body was inside. Marcel Haggerty, a ranch hand who'd worked for her family for four decades. Someone had murdered him. Sliced him up with a butcher knife.

"You don't have to do this," Seth reminded her again when he pulled to a stop next to a pair of police cruisers and the CSI van. Yet another car was parked next to it.

So many people.

So many memories.

She'd been eight years old when her father's blood had been found here. Only eight when her world had come crashing down around her. Some of those memories continued to crash right now. It was the same sickening dread that she got every time she laid eyes on the cabin. Her imagination was too good, and Shelby could almost see the nightmarish struggle that had left her father dead.

"You don't have to do this," Seth repeated. This time there was a bite to his voice, probably because he'd seen the color drain from her face.

"I want to ID the body. I owe Marcel that."

"You can't actually go in the cabin anyway. It's a crime scene. And you might not be able to see enough to do the ID."

Part of her wished that she wouldn't see *enough*, but Shelby had the sickening feeling that she would see a lot more than she wanted. "I'm doing this," she insisted.

Judging from the look Seth gave her, he still didn't approve, but he didn't stop her. In fact, he stayed right by her side, giving her the moral support she needed but wasn't sure she wanted from him. He probably didn't want to give that moral support, either, but their shared situation had broken down barriers between them.

So had that kiss.

Barriers that she needed in place to keep her sanity.

Probably Seth's sanity, too, making her wonder: Deep down beneath the history and the danger, how did he truly feel about the kiss?

How did *she* feel about it?

She was already starting to doubt what she'd believed for twenty-three years—that Jewell had killed her father. And Shelby didn't want those doubts to gain a foothold because of this insane attraction to Seth.

They made their way to the cabin. Shelby could smell wildflowers and hear the water in the nearby creek. The creek where her father's bone fragments had been found.

Yes, there were a lot of bad memories here.

The *bad* went up a significant notch when

Seth and she stepped into the doorway of the cabin. The place was just one small room with an attached bath, and even though the sheriff and the ME took up a lot of the space, Shelby had no trouble seeing the bed. Or the body that was sprawled out there.

Someone had put a mask of her father's face on him.

The ME lifted the mask for just a second, and Shelby saw that it was indeed Marcel.

It felt as if someone sucked all the air from her lungs, and even though she didn't show any outward signs of that, Seth must have sensed it because he took hold of her arm and moved her back on to the porch.

"Who's doing this?" she managed to say. Shelby wanted to scream. To run. But most of all, she just wanted this sick monster caught and punished.

"We'll find him and stop him," Seth said. "Or *her*."

It took Shelby a moment to realize why he'd added that *her*. Then she saw the woman stepping from a car.

Annette Prior.

It'd been several years since Shelby had seen the woman, but she hadn't changed or seemingly aged a bit. With her sleek blond hair tumbling to her shoulders, ample curves and expensive clothes, she looked like a celebrity and no-where close to fifty. However, her forehead was bunched up as if she was upset about something.

"Why are you here?" Seth demanded. Clearly not a friendly greeting. Probably because despite her alibi, Annette was still a suspect in his mind.

Annette's eyes narrowed a bit, her only reaction, before she turned her attention to Shelby. "I heard the news. Is it true? Is Marcel really dead?"

Shelby nodded and tried to stave off the images of his butchered body. "How'd you find out?"

When Annette got closer, Shelby could see her smeared mascara and reddened eyes. Annette had been crying. "It's all over town. Someone called to tell me, but I had to see for myself."

Seth made a skeptical sounding *humph.* "Why are you here?" he repeated.

Annette folded her arms over her chest and gave Seth a how-dare-you stare. "Marcel was a friend, and I wanted to make sure everything was being done to catch the monster who did this to him."

"Your friend?" Shelby challenged. She ran her gaze over Annette's cream-colored silk top and skirt. Considering that Marcel was a ranch hand, it didn't seem as though he'd have much in common with Annette. Still, Annette had been crying.

"Yes, my friend," Annette verified in a crisp tone. "We spoke at least once a month on the phone and met for lunch occasionally."

Seth glanced at Shelby to see if she knew any of this, but she had to shake her head.

"Last time Marcel and I talked," Annette went on, "he mentioned that your mother was in a psychiatric hospital. It's good to hear Carla's finally getting help for her mental problems. Please tell her I wish her the best."

Now it was Shelby's eyes that narrowed. "No way will I mention you to my mother."

Though it was true about the psychiatric hospital. Equally true that her mother had issues she needed to work out. But her mother didn't needed to hear that Shelby had seen one of the women Whitt had slept with. It'd be like rubbing salt in a still-open wound.

"After my father died, my mother found letters you'd written to him," Shelby explained. "Letters begging him to leave my mother. I'm thinking she wouldn't be very receptive to anything you have to say, especially any well wishes."

And even though Shelby and her mother didn't see eye to eye on a lot of things, they agreed Annette had tried her best to be a home wrecker. Of course, Jewell and Meredith fell into that same category, too.

"I'm not the enemy," Annette said, drawing Shelby's attention back to her. "We both know who the enemy is." And with that, Annette looked at Seth.

No doubt because Jewell was the one with the enemy label. Apparently the zinger that Annette had flung about Carla wasn't enough. Now the woman had to shoot arrows at Jewell through Seth.

But Jewell hadn't committed this latest murder.

Nor had she killed the other two and put masks on their faces. However, Annette could have done that.

Well, maybe.

"I'm surprised you could find your way out here," Shelby tossed out. "This cabin isn't exactly on the beaten path."

Annette didn't respond to that, but her gaze drifted to the cabin. "I was here once with your father. I didn't go inside," she quickly added. "When I spent nights with Whitt, I preferred a…more upscale accommodation."

"Then, why were you here at the cabin?" Seth asked, sounding very much like the FBI agent he was. "Because I don't remember you mentioning that during any of your interviews."

"No?" Annette certainly didn't seem concerned that it was something she'd omitted. "Must have slipped my mind. But as I said, I didn't even go inside the place. Whitt came here to pick up something, and I merely rode out here with him before we headed off to dinner."

Annette might be telling the truth. After all, her DNA hadn't been found inside. Still, there was plenty about the woman that Shelby didn't trust, and she didn't think that distrust was solely because Annette had been her father's mistress.

"I'd like to see Marcel's body," Annette said. New tears watered her eyes. "To say goodbye."

"Not possible," Seth answered. "The ME and sheriff are in there right now, and the scene's being processed."

"But you were just inside," she argued. "I saw you in the doorway when I drove up."

Seth tapped the badge on his belt to give her a reminder she didn't need—that he was the law. "Shelby looked inside so she could identify the body."

Which hadn't been necessary since Cooper had recognized Marcel. Still, it'd been something Shelby had had to do.

Annette blew out a long breath. "Can you call me when I can see the body?" she asked, pulling a business card from her purse. She handed it to Seth. "And can I have your number, as well?

Just in case I remember something about Marcel that you might want to know."

It wasn't a totally out-there request since Seth was an FBI agent, but again Shelby questioned the woman's motive. Why would Annette want to get in touch with Seth rather than someone in the sheriff's office?

After staring at her for several more seconds, Seth finally took out a business card and handed it to her. "Don't count on seeing Marcel before the funeral. You're not family or law enforcement, so there's no reason for you to view the body."

"No reason other than saying goodbye to a friend," Annette snapped. She looked at Seth's card and stuffed it into her purse. "I didn't want to have to wait to say my goodbyes at the funeral."

It seemed petty to try to ban Annette from doing that, but since Shelby's mother also might attend, maybe Marcel's family would agree to a private service.

Annette started to leave but then stopped. When she turned back around, she looked at Seth. "I don't suppose you know why Jewell wanted to see Marcel?"

Because Seth's arm was right against hers, Shelby felt him tense. "What are you talking about?" he asked.

Annette didn't smile, but it was close. "Jewell didn't tell you? Interesting."

Seth took a step closer to Annette. "Tell me what?"

"Marcel said Jewell's lawyer had called him, that she wanted Marcel to visit her at the jail so they could chat. Oh, well." Annette gave a dismissive wave of her hand, which, of course, didn't dismiss anything. "Since Jewell's lawyer told Marcel that it was important that she speak to him, I just figured she would have mentioned it to you. Since you're her stepson and all."

And with that new zinger, Annette got in her car and drove away.

"You really believe Jewell wanted to talk to Marcel?" Shelby asked him.

A muscle flickered in Seth's jaw. He stormed toward the car so fast that Shelby had to run to catch up with him. "I'm not sure, but I'm about to find out."

Chapter Seven

Seth hated the county jail. Hated that his mother was locked away in it. Now he had a new reason to hate it.

Because he was going to have to ask his mother about Annette's allegations.

If Jewell had truly asked Marcel to see her just days before he was murdered, then Seth needed to find out why she'd wanted to talk to him. Since anything he asked would likely sound like an accusation, he was bracing himself for a conversation he didn't want to have.

Especially a conversation that would take place in front of Shelby.

Seth had considered dropping her off at the sheriff's office, but Cooper and his deputies had their hands full—again. Three dead bodies in less than twenty-four hours, and the two kidnappers who could give them answers were still nowhere to be found.

"You can wait with the guards if you want,"

Seth suggested to Shelby as they went into the visitation area.

"After what happened last month, no thanks."

Yeah. He got that. Last month, a rogue guard had tried to kill Shelby's brother, Aiden, and Jewell's half sister, Kendall, when they'd come to visit Jewell. There'd been a thorough investigation, and several guards had been replaced, but the memory was still fresh enough to put Seth, and apparently Shelby, on edge.

"Besides, I want to see Jewell," Shelby added. "And yes, I know she won't be friendly to me. Still, I want to hear what she has to say about Marcel."

Seth had figured that was what Shelby would want, and the truth was he wasn't comfortable having her out of his sight. And no, it wasn't because of that stupid kiss. It was because someone was clearly gunning for her.

Someone who thought she was a traitor.

Or maybe it was Hance just using that traitor label to throw suspicion off himself. If so, it was working. If something happened to Shelby now, the cops likely would think it was tied to her father's murder.

Not to Hance.

Once Seth had some answers from his mother, he really needed to search for anything in this investigation that would give them a much-needed break. That way he could put Hance, Annette, Meredith or anyone else involved behind bars so Shelby would be safe.

Shelby's phone dinged the moment they sat down at the visiting table. "It's a text from my brother," she said reading from the screen. "He's notified our mother of Marcel's death. She wants to come home for the funeral."

Seth didn't know a lot of the details as to why Carla had committed herself to a mental hospital, but this wasn't the ideal time for a homecoming. Especially since the funeral and trial would be around the same time.

"You think it's wise for her to be here?" Seth asked.

Shelby shrugged. "Probably not, but I doubt I'll be able to talk her out of it. I got my hardheadedness from her." She added a smile. A real one. She probably didn't know that it lit up her whole face and made Seth wish they had more things for her to smile about just so he could see it again.

But any smile possibilities were cut short when the guard escorted his mother into the room.

Jewell managed a smile, as well. A thin one. She was too pale again. Too thin, as well. And the stress of being here was starting to show. She took a seat behind the thick Plexiglas that separated them, and once he got a good look at her eyes, he could tell that she'd been crying.

"Seth," she said. "Shelby." She extended the smile to Shelby. "I heard about what happened. I'm so sorry. Are you both okay?"

"We're fine," Seth answered, but all three of them knew that was a lie. His mother no doubt could see the worry on his face. "Did you hear that Marcel Haggerty was murdered?"

Fresh tears came to Jewell's eyes, and she nodded. "One of the guards told me. It's true? Did someone stab him in Whitt's cabin?"

"Yes." And now for the question that might make those tears even worse. "We ran into Annette Prior at the cabin, and she said you'd asked to speak to Marcel."

There was just a quick blink of surprise. "Oh," Jewell said on a rise of breath. "And you think my request to see him has something to do with his murder?"

"Does it?" Shelby snapped.

Jewell pulled back her shoulders. "I don't think so. Unless…"

"Unless?" Seth pressed when she didn't continue. Mercy, he hoped this wasn't anything he didn't want to hear.

"Unless someone thought Marcel might tell me something I shouldn't know," Jewell finally said.

Obviously, that wasn't the answer Shelby wanted, because she huffed. She probably wanted Jewell to make a full confession not only to Whitt's murder but also to hiring someone to orchestrate these attacks. But Seth knew Jewell wouldn't do anything to put him or her other children in harm's way.

So what was going on here?

"Why'd you want to see Marcel?" he asked.

Jewell paused. A long time. "Marcel and I were friends back in school, and we've stayed somewhat friendly over the years. Phone calls, Christmas cards, that sort of thing. I just wanted to see him before the trial started."

Hell. She was holding something back. He'd had plenty of experience with suspects and witnesses doing that during interviews. His mother's shoulders were still stiff. She was dodging his gaze. And she was nibbling on her bottom lip.

"I don't remember you ever talking about Marcel," Seth pointed out.

"Well, I didn't exactly talk a lot about my old life here in Sweetwater Springs."

No. She hadn't. In fact, he'd known it was too sore a subject to bring up so he hadn't. Maybe that'd been a huge mistake.

Shelby moved to the edge of her chair, getting

closer to the Plexiglas barrier. "Did you kill my father?" she came right out and asked.

Normally, this would be when he would have told anyone asking that question to back off. He would have protected Jewell at all cost, but Seth wanted to hear what she had to say.

Jewell didn't dodge Shelby's gaze. "Would you believe me if I said no?"

"No. But I'd *want* to believe you."

His mother smiled. "Because of Seth."

Oh, man. He hadn't wanted his mother to pick up on that, and once again, Seth cursed that blasted kiss.

"There's nothing going on between us." Shelby cursed, too, out loud. "All right, maybe there is, but it's something that shouldn't be going on."

Seth couldn't agree more. Would that stop him from kissing her again?

Probably not.

But at least he would know it was another mistake before he jumped right into it.

"And whatever's going on between Seth and me doesn't affect what I have to do to get to the truth," Shelby continued. "I need to find out who killed Marcel and those other two people. I need to know who thinks I'm a traitor and why people are dying because of me."

Jewell moved closer, as well. "I honestly don't know, but please believe me, if I had a way to stop this, I would. Not just for my son's safety but for yours."

Their gazes held for a long time, and Shelby finally nodded. "Thank you." And it sounded genuine. She stood, rubbed her hands along the sides of her jeans. "I need to get out of here."

"Take care of her," Jewell whispered to Seth. "Take care of yourself, too."

Seth and Jewell exchanged their usual I-love-yous and goodbyes, and since Shelby was practically bolting from the reception area, he went after her. He was slowed down some because he had to stop to retrieve his gun, so he didn't catch up with her until she was already at the front entrance.

When Shelby looked back at him, she also had some tears in her eyes. Tears that she quickly swiped away.

"I didn't want her to be that nice," she said.

Seth understood that. It was easier to make Jewell out to be a monster if she acted like one. But she never had. "Come on. We'll stop by the sheriff's office and see if there's any new information, and then I can take you home."

She huffed. "Take me home," Shelby repeated. "And then you can stash me away at some safe house. But I don't want to be stashed away, Seth. I want to find out who's killing these people."

"I want to find that out, too," he assured her

as they stepped outside. "But not at the risk of getting you killed."

He expected an argument, and one was definitely brewing, but movement near the truck he'd used to drive to the jail caught his attention.

"What is it?" Shelby asked.

Seth pulled her behind him and drew his gun. Normally, the sight of someone near his vehicle wouldn't have sent his adrenaline soaring, but after three murders he wasn't taking any chances.

Only a handful of vehicles were in the small parking lot. This area was reserved for visitors. The guards' parking area was off to the right.

It took a few moments before the person moved again, and Seth finally saw the man. Tall, wearing dark clothes. A baseball cap partially obscured his face. He was right next to the truck but ducked when he spotted Seth.

Definitely not a good sign.

"Go back inside and wait with the guards," Seth told Shelby, and then he started toward the man.

However, Seth had only made it a few steps when he heard a sound he definitely didn't want to hear.

A blast. Not from a gunshot, either.

It was much louder. And the truck exploded in a fireball.

The impact threw Seth back, and he landed right against Shelby. That was when he figured out she hadn't gone back in the building after all. That she was outside where she could be an easy target.

Since Seth was already falling anyway, he pulled Shelby to the ground with him and tried to cover her as best he could. Hell. Here she was, right back in the middle of danger.

"He's getting away," Shelby said, trying to lift her head. She pointed in the direction of the flames that had engulfed the truck.

Yes, the moron was definitely getting away. Or rather trying to. Seth levered himself up, took aim and fired. With the bomber on the run, Seth had known it would be a difficult shot, but the bullet slammed into the guy's shoulder, and he tumbled to the ground.

"Wait here," Seth told Shelby. "And this time I mean it." He tossed her his phone. "Get inside and call the county sheriff's office. Get someone out here right now."

Once Seth was certain Shelby was inside, he hurried after the man he'd just shot. He wasn't hard to find. The guy was on the ground twenty feet or so on the other side of the flaming truck. He was moaning and clutching his arm. Certainly not a pro because even though the injury didn't look life threatening, he wasn't doing much to get away.

"Don't shoot me again," the man snarled. "I surrender."

Seth went closer, keeping his gun aimed at him, while he kept watch around him. Not just for another attacker but to make sure Shelby stayed put.

"Who are you?" Seth demanded.

"Norris Strand." The guy groaned, added some profanity. "I need an ambulance now."

He did, and the sheriff's office would dispatch one. For now, though, Seth wanted some answers. The name didn't mean anything to Seth, nor did he recognize the guy's face.

"Why'd you blow up the truck?" Seth asked.

The man shook his head. "The timer malfunctioned."

It didn't take long for that to sink it, and it didn't sink in well. This idiot hadn't meant for the explosive device to go off until Shelby and Seth were inside the truck. It was supposed to have killed them.

Seth had to get his teeth unclenched before he could speak, and he put the gun right to Strand's head. "Who hired you to do this?"

Strand looked away as if he might dodge the question, but Seth moved his gun slightly and pulled the trigger. The bullet slammed into the ground right next to the guy's head.

"Are you crazy?" Strand yelled.

"At the moment, yes. Now tell me who hired you, or the next shot might not go in the dirt." It was a bluff, but as angry as Seth was, he figured he didn't sound too stable.

In the distance, Seth heard the sound of police sirens. It wouldn't be long now before the county deputies arrived.

Seth took aim again. "Who hired you?" he repeated.

"A man," Strand finally said.

Seth fired another shot, this one even closer to Strand's ear than the last one. "Who?" Seth yelled. "I want a name, and I want it now."

Strand made a strangled, whimpering sound and put his hands over his ears. "He never said, but I recognized his picture from the newspapers. It was Marvin Hance."

Of course.

He wasn't exactly surprised, but Seth was unnerved that this idiot had given up his boss so easily. Maybe this was some kind of setup, but he'd take what he could get. It was enough to toss Hance back in jail and keep him there for a while.

Seth stepped back when two deputies came barreling out of a cruiser. Both of them recognized Seth, probably because he'd bugged them enough about his mother's trial. The deputies trained their guns on the wounded man.

"Anybody with him?" Deputy Hawks asked Seth.

"No one that I saw, but he said he's working for Marvin Hance."

Seth left it at that, figuring if the deputy couldn't get Hance in fast enough for questioning, then Seth would call in the FBI. After all, this piece of dirt had just tried to kill a federal agent.

Deputy Hawks glanced back at the ambulance that had come to a stop in the parking lot and then at Shelby who was making her way toward them. Since Seth didn't want her near Strand or the fire, he ran toward her, catching on to her arm and pulling her back inside.

There wasn't a drop of color left in Shelby's face, and she held out his phone. "It's Cooper," she said, her voice barely a whisper. "They found another body."

A hoarse sob tore from her mouth, and Shelby practically tumbled into his arms. "This time, it's a woman," she added. "And she was murdered in my house."

Chapter Eight

Shelby got just a glimpse of the latest murder photos before Sheriff Cooper McKinnon hit the button on his computer to hide them.

But a mere glimpse was more than enough.

It was definitely the work of this sick killer. A dead woman wearing a mask of Shelby's face. This time, though, it felt even more personal since the woman had been murdered in Shelby's bed. It was also personal since this latest victim was one of their suspects in the attacks.

Meredith Bellows.

Mercy, when was this going to end?

Seth slipped his arm around her waist and eased her away from Cooper's computer. As he'd done during their last visit to the sheriff's office, he had her sit in a chair next to a deputy's desk while he finished yet another round of calls. This time it was to have someone bring in Hance, and maybe unlike the other visit, they'd actually get a murder confession from him.

All those people were dead because someone apparently wanted to get back at her. She couldn't be responsible for another death. She just couldn't be. She already felt ready to shatter into a million little pieces, and anything else would cause her to go right over the edge.

Seth finally finished his call and came closer to her. His black suit was covered with dust and dirt, probably a result of when he'd pulled her to the ground in the parking lot after the truck exploded. However, unlike her, he didn't appear ready to lose it. He just looked focused and angry.

Good.

Maybe that anger and focus would help them find this killer.

"Deputy Hawks is at the hospital with Strand while he's getting stitched up," Seth explained. "Strand's still claiming that Hance is the one who hired him."

"You don't believe him?" Shelby asked.

"I want to believe him, but Strand isn't exactly trustworthy." Seth groaned, scrubbed his hand over his face. "The CSI just confirmed the timer on the firebomb malfunctioned. That's why it went off when it did."

Even though her thoughts were a tangled mess, Shelby still had no trouble working that out. If the timer hadn't malfunctioned, Seth and she would have been inside the truck when it burst into flames.

"Strand intended to kill us," she concluded.

Seth made a sound of agreement, and even though Shelby didn't need proof of just how on edge they were, she got it when someone opened the front door of the sheriff's office. Seth stepped in front of her, and in the same motion, he put his hand over his gun. Ready to draw. But it wasn't the threat his body was clearly prepared for. However, it was someone that Shelby wasn't up to seeing.

Her mother.

Carla hurried in, her arms open, and she headed straight for Shelby. Her mother's cheeks were flushed, maybe because of the heat. Maybe because she'd been in a rush to get there. Too bad it was a waste of time. And more. This might make her mother's mental state even worse. Thankfully, she wasn't alone. Carla's psychiatrist, Dr. Joanne Wilks, came in right behind her.

"I heard about the attacks," Carla said, pulling Shelby into a hug. "About the murders, too. And I demanded that Dr. Wilks bring me to see you."

Shelby and her mother hadn't exactly had a picture-perfect relationship, especially after her father's murder. But for now Carla just seemed like a worried mom.

"Your mother can't stay long," the doctor clarified. "She needs to get back for her therapy sessions. She just wanted to see you."

Shelby doubted the therapy sessions were that pressing, but the doctor probably didn't want Carla in this stressful situation any longer than necessary.

"We're okay," Shelby assured her mother. Something she'd been lying about a lot lately.

"But Marcel isn't." Carla started to sob and dropped her head on Shelby's shoulder.

Seth moved closer as if he could help, but he must have realized there wasn't much he could do. However, Shelby noticed his movement had snagged her mother's attention because Carla pulled back and looked at him.

"You're Jewell's stepson," she said. Not quite an accusation, but close.

"I am." Unlike Carla's tone, his held no hint of a bad attitude.

Her mother looked him over from head to toe. "I'd heard that you were easy on the eyes."

Really? Her mother was bringing up Seth's looks at a time like this?

"Easy on the eyes," Carla repeated to Shelby in an almost secretive whisper. "And with you two being thrown together like this, I can understand why you'd let him jump in front of you like that."

Oh. So that was where this was going.

"Seth has saved my life multiple times," Shelby volunteered just in case her mother was about to launch into some kind of tirade against Jewell and anyone associated with her.

But clearly that was not where Carla was headed.

No.

Did her mother see this "thing" that was going on between Seth and her? Shelby hoped not, because she'd never hear the end of it.

Carla swallowed hard before she looked up at Seth again. "Don't let this monster hurt Shelby."

"I won't." Seth didn't hesitate, either, but his gaze went from her mother to the front of the building. To the man who was stepping from his car.

"Marvin Hance," her mother said, following Seth's gaze. Now there was plenty of venom in her voice. "Why is he here? Is he responsible for what's happening?"

"Possibly," Seth and Shelby said in unison. As he'd done with Shelby earlier, Seth stepped in front of Carla and her.

"We should be going," Dr. Wilks insisted. Probably because she sensed this meeting would only add to her patient's stress levels.

But Carla didn't budge, even when the doctor took hold of her arm. She stared at Hance. Nope, it was a glare. And Carla would have launched herself at Hance if both Seth and Dr. Wilks hadn't held her back.

Carla cursed him, calling him a string of vicious names, but it only caused Hance to smile. "You're high-strung like your daughter," he said.

Hance turned that sick smile on Shelby. "You know, if you want to keep seeing me, all you have to do is ask. You don't have to do it under the pretense of accusing me of another crime."

"No pretense," Seth insisted. He motioned for the doctor to get Carla moving, and she did. He waited until they were out of the building before he continued. He also moved in front of Shelby so that Hance couldn't see her. "Sheriff McKinnon here is going to question you about your connections to the person who tried to kill Shelby and me."

Shelby looked over Seth's shoulder to see if Hance had a reaction to that. He didn't, but he smiled at her again, causing Seth to huff.

"You can handle this?" Seth asked the sheriff, and when Cooper nodded, Seth's attention went to Colt. "Could you follow Shelby and me? I'd like to get her out of here."

Now Hance had a reaction. "What? You don't think your girlfriend can handle being in the room with me?"

Seth didn't respond. Well, not verbally, but

Shelby could practically feel the anger boiling inside him.

"Shelby," Hance tried again. "You're going to let Seth call the shots here? That's not like you. Where's the tough reporter who's been hounding me for months?"

Since Hance was clearly becoming agitated by Seth's silent treatment, Shelby went with it, too. She ignored him, though it was hard to do, and she walked with Seth and Colt to the door.

"That's it?" Hance shouted. "You start a mess and then just leave?"

Hance moved as if to reach for her, but the look Seth gave him could have frozen the desert.

"Let me know if he confesses," Seth said to Cooper, and he got her out of there. Not quickly. They strolled out as if they didn't have a murder suspect trying to goad them into a fight.

"You don't bring out the best in him," Colt mumbled as they walked to their vehicles. "So where am I following you?"

"The McKinnon ranch," Seth answered. That got Shelby's eyes widening, and it earned him a "what the heck?" look from Colt.

"I'm a thousand percent sure that's a bad idea," Shelby told Seth.

Did he listen? Of course not. Seth got them in a borrowed cruiser and headed toward the ranch with Colt following behind them in his truck.

"I needed to get you out of there," Seth explained to her. "Hance was enjoying that way too much. He's a sociopath, and he's getting off on seeing you in pain."

She couldn't argue with any of that, but Shelby could argue with the direction they were heading. "The McKinnons aren't going to want me on their ranch."

"True," he agreed. "But Roy won't turn you away. Not when he realizes you're in danger. Besides, we'll be in the guesthouse, not under the same roof as the others."

That didn't settle down her nerves one bit. "For how long?"

"Until I can make other arrangements, which I'll start working on right away, I don't want to use FBI channels because Hance still has plenty of connections. Connections that might accidentally leak the location of a safe house. I'd rather make the arrangements myself, and not while we're in the sheriff's office."

"You don't trust Cooper?" she asked.

He didn't exactly jump to say yes, something he probably would have done just a day or so ago. "The fewer people who know where we are, the better."

Shelby was all for that, but she couldn't stop the knot from forming in her stomach when Seth took the final turn to Sweetwater Ranch.

She hadn't been here since she was a kid, and the place had certainly changed. Three new houses were scattered around the property. Shelby had heard enough talk to know they belonged to Cooper, Colt and Seth's sister Rosalie and her husband. Shelby's sister, Laine, and her husband, Tucker, lived in another house that once had belonged to their grandfather.

All the McKinnons were coming home to roost.

That knot in Shelby's stomach got worse when she spotted the people on the porch of the main house.

Roy and Seth's sister Rayanne.

Seth parked the cruiser next to the guesthouse and waved at Colt to let him know he could go back to the station. Part of Shelby wished she could go with him because the idea of facing Hance suddenly seemed like the lesser of two evils. Especially considering the way Rayanne was glaring at her.

Seth didn't dodge that glare. He walked toward Roy and Rayanne, and Shelby was more than a little surprised when Roy smiled at her. And it seemed genuine.

"I'm sorry about the latest trouble," Roy said. "You're welcome to stay as long as you need."

It was a generous offer. One that Shelby certainly hadn't expected. The generosity, however, didn't extend to Rayanne. Seth's sister was megapregnant, and she had her hands on her huge belly and a big scowl on her face.

"Play nice," Seth said to Rayanne, and he brushed a kiss on her cheek. "How's my nephew?" He rubbed his hand on her stomach.

"As hardheaded as his uncle," Rayanne snarled, giving most of that snarl to Shelby.

"Rayanne's two days past her due date," Roy provided. "The doctor said she should walk, and I think she's a little tuckered out. Plus, she's craving ice cream, and we're out, so she's waiting on her husband to get back from the grocery store."

Rayanne made a yeah-right sound. "I'm not sporting this expression because I'm tuckered out or craving mint chocolate chip. I'm riled because my hardheaded brother brought Whitt Braddock's daughter here."

"Shelby's not responsible for what went on with Whitt," Roy said. "And I think Seth will breathe a lot easier if she's here, where she's safe. That means you'll breathe easier, too, since he'll be safe, as well."

Rayanne probably wanted to disagree with that, but then she huffed, her gaze going over Seth's dirty, torn suit. The dirt and the tears he'd gotten because someone had tried to kill them again.

"Just be careful," Rayanne finally said to Seth.

The warning might not have just been for the danger, either, because Rayanne volleyed a few glances between Shelby and him.

Mercy, were she and Seth wearing some kind of unwanted-attraction sign that others could see? Her mother had certainly picked up on it. Jewell, too. Now maybe Rayanne.

Roy slid his arm around Rayanne's waist and got them walking again. Seth did the same to Shelby and took her into the guest cottage. The place wasn't big: a living room–kitchen combo, two bedrooms and a bath. And it seemed even smaller when Seth stepped inside to join her.

"There's water and sodas in the fridge," he said, heading straight for one of the bedrooms. He shucked off his dirty jacket along the way.

Even though her throat was as dry as dust, Shelby sank down on the sofa instead. Too bad it gave her an unobstructed view of Seth, since he didn't shut the bedroom door. His holster and shirt came off next. Then he reached for the zipper on his pants.

That didn't help her dry throat.

Seth stopped, and as if suddenly remembering that he wasn't alone, looked back at her. "Sorry."

Shelby tried to shrug to make it seem like no big deal. It was, though. Seeing a half-naked Seth only reminded her body that she wouldn't mind seeing him completely naked.

Wouldn't mind more of those kisses, either.

Thankfully, that set off some huge warning bells in her head, and she forced herself to tear her gaze from him. To give herself something else to do, she picked up a photo album from the coffee table and thumbed through it.

It was a family album. Specifically, photos of Seth, Rosalie and Rayanne as children. In nearly all the shots Seth was riding a horse in what appeared to be various rodeo competitions.

And there was Jewell, of course.

In several photos she was standing next to a man in a wheelchair. He was the spitting image of Seth.

"Rosalie brought that album with her when we came to the ranch," Seth said. He came out of the bedroom wearing clean black pants. Zipped at that. No shirt, though he did have one and his badge in his hands. "Anything wrong?" he asked.

She was gawking at him again but managed to shake her head. What the heck? She might as well just spill what Seth already figured she was thinking.

"You know you tick all the boxes for 'hot guy,'" Shelby said. "Even my mother noticed. Half the women in town are fantasizing about you. The other half are too young or old to fantasize."

The corner of his mouth lifted. "Is that why you kissed me, because you think I'm hot?"

"Of course." But then she rethought that. "Or maybe it's because in addition to those hot-guy boxes, you're a bona fide lifesaving hero."

He motioned to the badge that he clipped to his belt. "It's part of the job."

Shelby motioned to his heart instead. "I think you would have saved my life even if you weren't wearing that badge."

Seth only shrugged. "You know, you tick all the hot boxes, too."

Thankfully, she was still seated or that might have sent her into his arms. She was so easily swayed around him. Too easily.

All right.

It was time for her to put some mental distance between them. "Is that your father?" she asked, tapping one of the photos of the man in the wheelchair.

He nodded, after several seconds of staring at her. "When I was just a baby, my mom and dad were mugged when they were at a cattle auction near San Antonio. My mother was killed, and the man shot my father, severing his spine."

"Sweet mercy." Her breath stopped for a moment. As part of her investigation into Jewell, Shelby had done a background check on Seth, but she hadn't delved into his childhood. "I'm so sorry."

"It was a long time ago." True, but she still heard the emotions in his voice.

"They caught the person who did this?" she asked.

But she had to repeat that "sweet mercy" when Seth shook his head.

Well, that explained why he'd become a lawman. He was out for justice. Justice that he probably knew he wouldn't get for his parents, since the crime had happened over thirty years ago. Still, it was one of those wounds that would never heal.

She knew a little about never-healing wounds herself.

Shelby looked at a few more pictures, the snapshots giving her a little summary of his life. Despite his father being in a wheelchair, they appeared to be a happy family. Heck, even surly Rayanne was smiling in some of the photos.

Then the shots changed.

Seth's father was no longer in any of the pictures. If she remembered correctly, he'd died when Seth had been twelve or so. The rest of the photos were of the ranch, horses and rodeo competitions.

Shelby looked up at him. Finally, he was

putting on his shirt. "So beneath the FBI suit, you're really a cowboy."

"Was. *Am*," Seth corrected. "I just bought the Bradley ranch not far from here. Once the trial is over, I'll move there and get back to what I love—working with the horses."

It was yet something else Shelby didn't know about him. "What about the FBI?"

"I'm assigned to the San Antonio office. That's close enough for me to commute."

Again, it was the first she was hearing about his plans. "You're staying in Sweetwater Springs?"

"Yeah." His gaze met hers. "What, this town isn't big enough for both of us?"

It would have been a cute joke if there hadn't been some truth in it. Shelby got to her feet slowly. "But what if Jewell's convicted?"

"Then, I'll still be close to Rayanne and Rosalie. They're both making their lives here."

Their lives, yes, and families of their own. Rosalie already had a daughter and Rayanne was about to make Seth an uncle again.

"But the Bradley place?" she remarked. "It's huge." Several thousand acres. And the house was more of a mansion than a ranch house. Since the previous owner was in jail for murder, Seth probably had bought it for a decent price, but it still would have been steep.

Which might happen very soon now.

Without letting go of her, Seth turned until she was sandwiched between the back of the sofa and him. Anchored in place. But neither stayed put. They adjusted, fighting to get closer. Struggling to get closer until Shelby finally got the contact that her body was screaming for. Seth's sex against hers.

Even though there were clothes between them, he didn't disappoint with the intimate contact. Nor did he stop the wildfire kisses on her neck and mouth.

Shelby was certain that she was ready to lose it and drag him off to bed when Seth suddenly stopped. In the blink of an eye, he moved away from her, switching from hot cowboy to Mr. FBI. Because she was so rattled, it took her a moment to realize what had caused the transformation.

His phone was ringing.

Everything came back to her when he pulled his phone from his pocket. Not just the fierce attraction but the really important stuff. Such as the fact they were in the middle of a multiple murder investigation, and the call—*any* call— could be critical.

"It's Annette," Seth said, glancing at the screen. He hit the speaker button on his phone.

"Seth, you have to help me," Annette insisted. Her words rushed together and were filled with a heavy breath. It sounded as if the woman was running.

"What's wrong?" Seth immediately asked.

"Help me," Annette repeated. "I'm near Whitt's cabin, and someone's trying to kill me. I'll meet you at the sheriff's office."

That was all Annette said before Shelby heard two other things that she didn't want to hear.

A gunshot followed by Annette's blood-chilling scream.

surprisingly level and calm. "I'm tired of your threats. Tired of you. So let's finish this in court."

At least that caused Hance's smirk to fade.

Since the guy was essentially a murdering bully, he probably got off seeing Shelby afraid. But Seth was betting Shelby was too numb to deal with anything Hance was trying to dish out.

Hance motioned for his attorneys to follow him, and he headed for the front door. However, he stopped when he reached the window. And Seth soon saw why.

Annette was running straight for the sheriff's office.

"Get out of here now," Seth warned Hance and his legal entourage.

No way did Seth want Hance around while he dealt with Annette. Seth practically shoved them out the door, and then he pushed Shelby behind him.

Cooper came rushing to the front, too, and drew his weapon.

Annette was wearing the same clothes she'd had on earlier when Seth had seen her at the cabin, but now there were smears of dirt on them. Dirt on her face, too. Her hair was a tangled mess, and she was hobbling. It took Seth a moment to realize she was doing that not because she was injured but because one of her heels had broken off.

She didn't have a gun in her hands, wasn't carrying a purse, and with that snug outfit, she probably wasn't carrying a concealed weapon. Still, Seth didn't intend to take any chances.

"Wait in Cooper's office," Seth told Shelby, and he paused until she was in the hall before he opened the door to let Annette in.

"Help me," Annette said, her voice a raw whisper. She practically tumbled into Seth's arms.

Seth handed her off to Cooper so he could take a quick look outside to make sure Annette hadn't brought hired guns with her. Or to see if she'd been followed by someone else's hired gun. But no one appeared to be lurking nearby waiting to attack. Still, Seth shut the door and continued to volley glances between Annette and outside.

After a closer look, Annette didn't appear to have any serious injuries, although there were a few small cuts and nicks on her face and arms. Judging from the bits of leaves and twigs in her hair, she'd run through the woods.

"What happened?" Seth demanded.

Cooper had the woman sit in one of the chairs, and he brought her a cup of water. Annette's breath was gusting, and she didn't even attempt to answer until she finished the entire cup.

"I went back to the cabin," she finally said.

"So I could see Marcel's body, to make sure it was really him."

Seth groaned. She was damn persistent when it came to seeing the remains of the ranch hand. The question was why?

A hoarse sob left her mouth, and tears slid down her cheeks. "Marcel shouldn't have died."

"Ditto for the other people who were murdered," Seth reminded her.

But judging from the way Annette shook her head, the tears and this grief were all for Marcel. Seth made a mental note to check and see if Annette and Marcel had been romantically involved. It would have definitely been a case of opposites attracting, but considering what was going on between Shelby and him, he figured just about anything was possible.

"What happened? Who attacked you?" Seth pressed. He motioned for Shelby to stay back when she started toward them. He might as well have saved his energy because Shelby didn't stop moving closer to them.

"I don't know," Annette said at the end of another sob. "I was in the woods near the cabin. I wanted to watch those investigators remove Marcel's body. But then I heard someone moving around behind me, and I spotted a man. He was armed and wearing a ski mask."

Seth stared at her, trying to figure out if this

was anywhere close to the truth. Annette was clearly shaken, but if she was the person behind the attacks, maybe she was shaken because something had gone wrong with her plan.

Something that wasn't supposed to have included Marcel's murder.

"Did this man say anything to you?" Shelby asked.

Annette shook her head. "He just pointed his gun at me, so I ran."

"You ran?" Seth repeated. "Why not just call out to the CSIs for help?"

"I wasn't that close to them. I'd been watching the cabin with binoculars, so I didn't think the CSIs would have time to get to me and stop the gunman."

They probably wouldn't have gotten to her in time. If Annette was telling the truth about her location. "What happened next?" Seth asked.

Annette motioned for another cup of water, which Cooper got for her, and she again finished it before speaking. "I kept running. I had a gun in my purse, and I tried to get it out, but I dropped it. I managed to grab my phone, and I'd programmed in your number from the business card you gave me."

Interesting. Since he'd given her the card only several hours earlier. "Why would you do that?"

"Because of what happened to Marcel. I

figured if this killer came after me, then you'd help me."

Seth wasn't sure why she would turn to him instead of the sheriff, but then he had a lot of questions when it came to Annette and these possible lies she was telling. "What happened after you called me?"

"You already know." Annette shuddered. "That's when the man fired a shot at me. I dropped my phone when I ran into a tree limb, and I kept running until I made my way here."

Seth glanced at Cooper to get his take on this. The CSIs had indeed reported the sound of a gunshot, and Seth had heard one when Annette had called him. That still didn't mean Seth believed her. Apparently, neither did Cooper.

Cooper moved in front of Annette, made eye contact. The kind of flat eye contact a lawman made with a suspect. "Why would this person want to kill you?"

"How should I know?" Annette threw her hands in the air. "Why would he want to kill Marcel?"

Seth didn't have an answer for that. Or for any of this insanity that was happening. And in this case, not knowing could keep Shelby and him right in the path of danger.

"I'll call an ambulance," Cooper said, taking out his phone. "Annette, you need to be checked out."

"I want protection if I leave here," Annette argued. "That man could come after me again."

Cooper was already short on manpower, but before he made the call for an ambulance, he phoned his night deputy and asked for the man to come in so he could accompany Annette to the hospital. That was Seth's cue to get moving, too. He was about to call the ranch hands again to ask them to escort Shelby and him back to the ranch.

But a black car caught Seth's attention.

It pulled to a stop directly in front of the sheriff's office with the passenger's side just a yard or so from the main entrance.

The windows were heavily tinted so he couldn't see inside. Not good. Apparently Annette was having the same thought.

"Oh, God. That gunman's coming to kill me," she blurted out, and headed for the back of the building. She ducked into one of the interview rooms and slammed the door shut.

Seth didn't bother to stop her, and even though he wanted Shelby to follow Annette's lead, he didn't especially want her left alone with the woman.

"Stay behind me," Seth warned her.

Shelby did, but she came up on her toes to

look over his shoulder. Both of them and Cooper had their attention fastened to the car door as it opened, and the driver stepped out.

A tall, wide-shouldered man wearing a white Stetson emerged. Beneath the hat, Seth could see their visitor's salt-and-pepper hair. Since the man kept his back to them for several moments, Seth had no idea who this was. Nor could he tell if the guy was armed.

The man finally turned, his gaze zooming right to the window where Cooper, Shelby and Seth were waiting. The corner of the man's mouth lifted into a half smile, and he started toward the front door. Not quickly. He was walking with a pronounced limp.

"Oh, mercy," Shelby said at the same moment that Cooper muttered, "What the hell?"

Shelby caught onto Seth's arm and dropped her weight against him. Clearly, something had spooked both Cooper and her, and once the man opened the door and Seth got a better look, he understood why.

He was looking at the face of a dead man. Or at least a man who was supposed to be dead.

Whitt Braddock.

SHELBY FELT AS if someone had punched her. All the air vanished from her lungs, and she heard herself make a strangled sound of shock.

Obviously, her mind and eyes were playing tricks on her.

Yes, that had to be it.

But any proof of that mirage or illusion vanished when the man walked inside the sheriff's office. She frantically studied his face, combing over every detail. It'd been twenty-three years since she'd last seen him, but there was no doubt about it.

This was her father.

Oh, God.

"Shelby," her father said, his attention going straight to her.

She looked at Seth and Cooper to see if they had any explanation for this, but along with keeping their guns drawn, they were volleying glances at her, apparently to see if she had any answers.

She didn't.

"How?" was all that Shelby managed to say, even though a dozen questions went through her head. But one question was by far the front-runner.

How was her father alive?

He came toward her as if to pull her into his arms. And she wanted that. Mercy, did she. As a kid, she'd fantasized that her father was still alive. She'd made up stories of his homecoming, but this real-life meeting didn't exactly live up to the fantasy.

Seth blocked him from coming closer to her. "Why the hell aren't you dead?" he snapped.

Whitt didn't acknowledge Seth. He kept his attention pinned to Shelby. "We need to talk. *Alone.*"

"That's not gonna happen," Seth insisted.

"But you are going to talk to me," Cooper added. "Start explaining *now.*"

Her father released a weary-sounding breath. "For a long time, I had amnesia."

Shelby wanted to latch on to that explanation. Because it meant he hadn't intentionally left her and the rest of his family. But there were the troubling words.

"For a long time?" she questioned.

Her father nodded. "I was injured. Lost a lot of blood, and I guess that caused my amnesia."

"That blood loss is what put Jewell behind bars," Seth said, his voice low and dangerous. Shelby hoped he wouldn't launch himself at her father. Cooper, too. But both Seth and Cooper were clearly fighting to rein in their rage.

"Start from the beginning," Shelby insisted.

Her father huffed. "Don't I at least get a hug from my baby daughter first?" He extended his arms, waiting.

Shelby let him wait. "Tell us what happened."

Even though there were more wrinkles on his face, more gray hair, too, his expression hadn't changed. He pulled his mouth into a flat line before he gave a conceding nod.

"Twenty-three years ago I met Jewell at the cabin." He pulled off his Stetson and sank down into a chair. "After we, well, finished, we had an argument, and she stormed out. Jewell was always high-strung so I figured she'd be back after she settled down a bit. I just stayed in bed, waiting for her, and I fell asleep. When I woke up, someone shot me."

"Jewell?" Cooper immediately asked.

But her father shook his head. "I'm not sure who it was. Maybe Jewell, maybe someone else. The curtains were pulled, and the room was dark. I only saw a shadowy figure before the bullet went into my chest. I lost consciousness, and when I came to, the person was gone, and I had both a gunshot and some stab wounds."

Shelby had no choice but to sit down, as well. "Why didn't you call someone? Why didn't you call Mom?"

"No phone. My attacker must have taken it. I managed to get up and get outside, but my truck was gone, too. I knew I was bleeding to death so I staggered to the creek, figuring the cold water would slow the bleeding. I fell in, and I must have floated or something because when

I came to, I was on the creek bank. An elderly woman found me and took care of me."

The images and thoughts were like wildfire in her head, and Seth must have realized she was about to lose it because he slipped his hand onto her shoulder. Her father didn't miss the gesture because his eyes widened, then narrowed, but Shelby was too shaken to deal with his reaction to Seth and her.

"An elderly woman?" Cooper barked. He didn't sound shaken. Just furious.

"I don't know who she was," her father insisted. "I faded in and out of consciousness for weeks. The woman didn't have a phone, not even electricity. She was in some hunting shack in the woods, and I remember her saying she was going to try to walk into town and get some help for me. She never returned."

"You have any idea who this woman is?" Seth asked Cooper.

Cooper holstered his gun. "No, and no woman came into town looking for medical help around that time. Plenty of people were searching for Whitt, and a woman claiming to have an injured man in her cabin would have alerted the hospital and the sheriff."

But that didn't mean the woman hadn't been real. There were plenty of remote areas in the county. Plenty of hunting cabins, too. Of course, that didn't mean any of this made sense.

"Keep talking," Shelby told her father. "What happened next?"

"About a week after the woman left, I ran out of food. Still didn't have a clue who I was or what'd happened to me, but I was stronger, so I took what little money she had lying around, left the cabin and started walking. When I made it to the road, I hitched a ride with a trucker who drove me to Laredo. I stayed in a homeless shelter until I was back on my feet."

"But you did get back on your feet." Shelby faced her father head-on. "How long did it take before you remembered who you were?"

He didn't dodge her gaze. Not physically anyway. But his mouth went flat again. "About six months."

Six months? Mercy, that felt like another punch to the gut.

"I was in a bad place," her father hurried to add. "I knew I'd screwed up my life and wanted a fresh start. I'd stashed away some money in offshore accounts. Money that no one else knew about. And I tapped into those accounts so I could start a new ranch. A new life. Something I don't expect you to understand."

Everything inside her was twisting and turning, and it felt as if someone had their hands around her throat choking her.

"But you expect me to forgive you?" she asked.

"No," he said. Then he repeated it several times. "I don't expect you to understand that I stayed away because I didn't want my attacker to come after me or my family again. I figured as long as I was near you, I'd put you in danger. But I'm back now." Whitt's attention shifted to Seth. "To stop this killer from hurting my baby daughter and to help Jewell get out of jail."

Certainly, it'd already occurred to Seth that his mother couldn't be guilty of murder. Not with the alleged murder victim right in front of them. But for Shelby it was just sinking in.

It didn't sink in well.

"You son of a bitch," Seth snapped. "You let Jewell sit in jail all this time. For nearly nine months—"

"I didn't know she'd been arrested," Whitt interrupted. "My ranch is out in the sticks, way down by the border, and I don't listen to the news. Don't even have a TV. When I finally saw the story in a newspaper, I knew I had to come back to Sweetwater Springs. I decided to come to the sheriff's office first. Glad I did, because otherwise I would have had to go looking for Shelby so I could talk to her face-to-face."

The words were right, the explanation maybe even plausible. *Maybe*. But something still didn't fit. "What about the bone fragment? It was found near the cabin, and DNA confirmed it was yours."

"Yes," he readily admitted.

Then Whitt lifted the leg of his jeans, and Shelby saw the metal prosthetic leg.

"I was in a bad car wreck about ten years ago, and my leg had to be amputated. I kept a piece of the bone as a stupid memento, but about six months ago, I realized it was missing."

"Missing?" Seth said, skepticism dripping from his voice. "You're sure you didn't use it to set up my mother?"

Whitt stood and met Seth eye to eye. "I wouldn't do something like that."

Shelby wanted to believe him. Sweet heaven, she wanted it more than her next breath. But all of it seemed tied up in a too-neat package.

"Does Mom know you're alive?" Shelby asked, standing, as well.

But he didn't get a chance to answer.

"Whitt?" Shelby heard someone say. Annette. The woman came out of the interview room, her hand flying to her mouth, and she bolted toward Whitt, throwing herself into his arms. "You're here."

That immediately set off alarms in Shelby's

head. Annette hadn't said "you're alive" but rather "you're here."

"You knew he wasn't dead." Seth added some harsh profanity to that accusation against Annette.

The woman certainly didn't deny it. She pressed a flurry of kisses to Whitt's cheek and probably would have continued those kisses to his mouth if Whitt hadn't gently moved her away.

Clearly disgusted with all this, Seth stepped to the side and put his gun back in his holster. "I need to make some calls."

Calls to his sisters and Jewell, no doubt. Since the murder charges would be dropped, Jewell would be set free.

And that meant for the past twenty-three years Shelby had believed a horrible lie.

That Jewell had murdered her father and robbed her, her mother and siblings of the life they should have had.

All a lie.

A lie perpetrated by her father. Maybe he was even lying about the amnesia. At this point, Shelby had to assume anything coming out of his mouth was a lie.

"Shelby," her father said, walking toward her again. "I know this is hard for you. You were always my little princess. But I've prayed that you'll eventually find it in your heart to forgive me."

"You actually pray?" she snapped. Yes, it was a petty dig, but right now there was zero chance of forgiveness. "My mother went crazy when you left. And you didn't just leave her. You left Aiden, Laine and me. We grew up without a father. Though in hindsight, that might have been better than the alternative."

That brought on another expression that she remembered. The anger flashed through her father's eyes, but she saw him quickly cover it. Maybe because he realized she had a good reason to be enraged. Or maybe because he knew his anger was only going to make this worse.

Thankfully, Cooper took over with the necessary questions. "How long have you known Whitt was alive?" he asked Annette.

"Not long," Annette said.

"A long time," Whitt disagreed, earning him an outraged huff from Annette. "I called her shortly after I regained my memory. Swore her to secrecy, though, so that's why she didn't tell anyone."

Cooper cursed, put his hands on his hips. "And it didn't occur to you that Annette could have been the one who tried to kill you in the cabin all those years ago?"

"I wouldn't try to kill him!" Annette howled.

"I love Whitt. Always have, always will. It must have been Jewell. Think about it. She hasn't said a word about being innocent, so you can bet she's the one who attacked Whitt and left him for dead."

Maybe Jewell had. But if so, it still wasn't murder, and considering all the other lies, Shelby figured it was time for her to give Jewell the benefit of the doubt. Any other doubts she had, she'd aim right at her father.

"I can't be sure if it was Jewell who attacked me," Whitt explained. "Like I said, the cabin was dark. Could have been Roy, I suppose. He wasn't exactly happy about his wife carrying on with me."

No, and neither was Annette. Even now, after all these years, the mention of it caused her eyes to narrow.

"My father had an alibi," Cooper insisted. "An eyewitness who saw him the day you were supposedly murdered."

Whitt shrugged, clearly not convinced about the alibi, or maybe he just wanted to muddy Roy's name a little.

"As much as Roy hated you," Shelby said to her father, "I suspect you felt the same way about him. How can we be sure you aren't just trying to set him up?"

That flare of temper went through her father's

eyes again. "I'll forgive you for implying that I had any part in the violence that went on that day. You're upset. I get that. But once you come to your senses you'll remember that someone wanted me dead all those years ago. Someone who's still killing."

And that did perhaps lead them back to Whitt's original attacker, but not necessarily back to Roy. Shelby remembered the kindness Roy had shown her by allowing her to come to the McKinnon ranch. No venom.

But she was seeing plenty of that venom in her father.

Just as she'd seen in Hance.

There was no way Hance could have been the one who'd tried to kill her father twenty-three years ago, but he certainly could be responsible for the recent murders and the attacks on Seth and her.

Of course, Shelby could say the same for Annette.

The woman was mostly lovey-dovey right now, but Shelby knew Annette had a mean streak. And an obsession with Whitt. Heaven knew what Annette would have done while carrying out that obsession.

"I need to call Aiden and Laine and tell them what's going on," Shelby said, turning away from her father. She had no choice. With her emotions boiling just beneath the surface, she might slap or curse him if she didn't give herself some space.

Shelby went to Colt's desk to make those calls, but the moment she stepped away, Cooper took some handcuffs from one of the other deputies' desk.

"Whitt Braddock and Annette Prior," Cooper said, "I'm placing you both under arrest."

"Arrest?" Whitt snapped. "You don't have any grounds to do that."

"Sure I do. I can hold you for suspicion of obstruction of justice for not coming forward when Jewell was arrested. It's the same for Annette."

Whitt's glare turned nasty. "That'll never hold up."

But her father was talking to himself because Cooper was already slapping the cuffs on him.

Chapter Ten

Seth had to force himself to stop pacing across the waiting room of the county jail. Hard to do, though, with his mind racing a mile a minute. When he'd woken up this morning he'd had no idea that this would become one of those life-changing days.

First, the attack on Shelby and him.

Whitt's return from the dead.

Now his mother would finally be released from jail.

Too bad the paperwork for that release was moving a lot slower than Seth wanted, but Jewell's sister, Kendall, and her lawyer were literally walking the paperwork through in the hope Jewell would be out in the next hour or so. That was why Roy, Rosalie, Rayanne, Rayanne's husband and Seth all had come to the jail to wait.

Shelby had come, too.

It was probably the last place on earth she wanted to be considering they had nearly been killed here after their last visit, but she hadn't wanted to stay at the sheriff's office with her father.

And Seth couldn't blame her.

Colt and Cooper were tied up with Whitt's and Annette's interrogations, but their other brother, Tucker, had called to say he'd be at the jail as soon as he wrapped up a case in San Antonio.

On the Braddock front, Shelby's brother, Aiden, was on his way to confront his dad. Aiden was the county sheriff, and Whitt was at the Sweetwater Springs sheriff's office— Cooper's jurisdiction since Cooper was the town's sheriff. Seth didn't expect that to be a friendly meeting, since it was common knowledge that there was no love lost between Aiden and his father.

Right now, the same could be said for Shelby and Whitt.

She was leaning her back against the concrete wall, no doubt using it for support, and she kept nibbling on her bottom lip.

"You should sit down," Seth suggested for the umpteenth time.

But she only shook her head and motioned toward Roy and his sisters, who were on the other side of the room. They were all seated at a round table normally used for visitors meeting with prisoners who'd been charged with lesser crimes and therefore required less security.

"You should be over there with them," Shelby said. "This is a day of celebration for all of you."

Seth stayed put. "I'm sorry. Not for my mother being set free. But I'm sorry your father did this to you and your family."

She tried to wave him off, but her breath broke, and because she likely had no choice, Shelby sank down into one of the chairs. The tears came. Tears that she'd no doubt been fighting since her father had walked back into her life. But this time she couldn't stop them. They streamed down her cheeks. She wiped them away only to have fresh ones return.

Seth gave a heavy sigh and dropped down next to Shelby, pulling her into his arms. The gesture earned him a grumble from Rayanne, but Seth ignored it.

"I can't believe he did this," Shelby whispered. She pressed her hand over her heart. "I grieved for him. Ached for him. Cried my eyes out over him. So did my mother. And all this time he was alive."

Shelby had left out the part about fighting for most of her life to bring his killer to justice. It had defined her. Been her obsession. Now she had to realize that her fight had been all for nothing. However, that did leave Seth with a huge problem.

Who the hell was killing people and putting those masks on their faces?

Who was trying to kill Shelby and him?

Hance was still on his suspect list. Annette, too. But now Seth had to add Whitt to the possible suspects.

Except that didn't make sense.

Why would Whitt want Shelby dead?

If there was a good answer for that, Seth couldn't come up with one. Unless...

"Whoever attacked your father all those years ago could have figured out he was alive and wanted to finish what he or she started." Seth was really just thinking out loud, but it seemed to strike a chord with Shelby because she stopped crying, paused, then nodded.

"A lot of people disliked my father," she added. She groaned. "Too many. We're talking bad blood over land deals, cattle sales and his extramarital affairs. Meredith, Annette and Jewell weren't the only ones he slept around with."

No, they hadn't been. Seth had done some digging to come up with possible suspects in the hopes of clearing Jewell's name, but it'd been hard to sort gossip from fact, and most of Whitt's lovers hadn't been willing to admit anything that would make them potential murder suspects.

"Once my mother's out of jail," Seth said, "we can start looking at some of Whitt's discarded lovers. Their husbands, too, since Whitt's attempted murder could have come at the hands of a jealous spouse."

If Whitt was telling the truth about the attack, that was.

With all the man's other lies, Seth figured Whitt could be lying about that, too. Heck, maybe Whitt had staged his attack so it would implicate Jewell. It could be the same for the bone fragment. Maybe there'd been no break-in, and Whitt had been the one to plant that bone so it would ensure Jewell's conviction.

But why?

Seth didn't have time to come up with an answer to that because his phone dinged, indicating he had a text message. It was from Cooper, who wanted Seth to call him back ASAP. Since the cell reception in this part of the jail was bad, he needed to step into the hall just off the security checkpoint.

"I'll be right back," Seth told his family, and he took Shelby by the arm to lead her out with him.

However, the moment they were out in the security area, Seth saw a man making a beeline toward them. County Sheriff Aiden Braddock,

Shelby's brother. When he reached Shelby, he immediately pulled her into his arms.

"You okay?" Aiden asked her.

The question caused her eyes to water again. No, she wasn't okay. But then, Aiden didn't appear to be, either. No tears for him, but Seth recognized the face of a riled man.

"Did you see Dad?" Shelby asked.

Aiden nodded. "Whitt's a sick bastard." And he hugged his sister even tighter.

Since Shelby needed to work this out with her brother, Seth stepped a few feet away to make the call to Cooper.

"This is a heads-up," Cooper said the moment he answered. "I'll have to release Whitt and Annette. They both lawyered up, and unless something drastic happens, they'll be released on bail in the next few minutes."

Seth groaned. "You gotta be kidding me." His groan obviously got Aiden and Shelby's attention, so he put the call on speaker.

"Wish I were kidding," Cooper continued. "Disappearing in itself isn't a crime unless it costs lots of money and resources to track a person down. Whitt has offered to pay for that. Plus, he never collected on any life insurance. I can charge him with impeding an investigation by not coming forward with the truth about being alive, but I'm sure his lawyers will argue that he didn't know Jewell was about to stand trial."

"He knew," Seth insisted.

"I agree, and I figure Whitt wanted her to sit in jail as long as possible so he could punish her for their relationship gone bad, but the bottom line is that it'll be hard to prove. Right now, the most he's looking at is probation. Maybe not even that unless I can find something else to pin on him."

Seth cursed. "Find something, *anything* to put his butt behind bars."

"Whitt's getting out of jail," Aiden said the moment Seth finished the call. He didn't wait for Seth to confirm it, and he cursed, too.

"Did Dad say anything to you that would make sense of all of this?" Shelby asked her brother.

Aiden shook his head. "No. But I only talked to him for a couple of minutes. I figured if I stayed much longer, I'd punch him, and Cooper would have to arrest me."

Shelby made a sound of agreement. "Someone needs to tell Mom."

"Laine's on her way to the mental facility to do that," Aiden explained. "She's arranged for the shrink to be with them."

Good, because Carla might need it, especially after she learned Annette had known Whitt was alive. But maybe Carla could help with finding some evidence that would put Whitt behind bars. Unless Carla wanted to take him back, that was. Seth figured that was a long shot, but Whitt did seem to have a way with women.

A thought that sickened Seth.

The door to the visiting room opened, and Rosalie stuck her head out, her attention zooming right to Seth. "They just brought Mom in."

"Has she been released?" Seth asked immediately.

"Not yet. But it shouldn't be long now. The guards are going to let her sit with us while the paperwork's still being processed." Rosalie turned to Shelby. "Come in, too. I told Mom you were here, and she wants to see you."

Shelby volleyed glances between Seth and her brother, and Aiden eased her toward the door. "Go ahead. Talk to Jewell," he said. "And give her my apologies. I'll do it myself in person after I find out what the hell's going on with Whitt."

"Call me if you find out anything we can use to throw him in jail," Seth insisted.

And despite the barked order, Aiden only nodded and brushed a kiss on his sister's cheek before he walked away.

"You don't have to apologize for anything your father did," Seth assured her, and he led Shelby back into the visitation room.

His mother was indeed there. Not behind the Plexiglas, either. She was standing in the room, hugging Rayanne and Blue, Rayanne's husband.

And Roy.

Seth wasn't immediately sure how he felt about that. After all, Roy had turned her and the twins out all those years ago. Still, if his mother could let bygones be bygones, then he'd have to try, as well. Especially since Roy had been nothing but civil to him since Seth had arrived at Sweetwater Ranch.

"Seth," Jewell said, going to him. She pulled both him and a hesitant Shelby into her arms. "I'm glad you're here."

"Wouldn't be anywhere else," Seth assured her.

When Jewell pulled back and their gazes met, he could see that she'd been crying. Happy tears, he hoped.

"I'm so sorry," Shelby whispered to her, and then she repeated it, louder, no doubt for Rayanne, Blue, Roy and Rosalie to hear.

"None of this was your fault," Jewell answered, and she managed a smile.

"I'll go check and see what's holding up the release paperwork," Blue volunteered, and headed out.

Jewell gave each one of them long looks.

Another smile. But the smile didn't quite make it to her eyes.

"Did you know Whitt was alive?" Shelby came out and asked.

Seth snapped toward her, angry that she would suggest such a thing. But then his stomach dropped to his knees when he saw the expression on his mother's face.

"Yes," Jewell answered.

The room went as silent as death.

On a weary sigh, Jewell sank down on one of the chairs at the table. She motioned for the others to do the same, and one by one, they did.

All except Seth.

He already didn't like the direction this conversation was taking, and he figured he was better off standing.

"What I'm about to say won't make things better," Jewell started. "And at this point I'm not even sure telling you is the right thing. Still, I'd rather you hear the truth from me rather than the lies Whitt will almost certainly tell you."

Oh, man. This is going to be bad.

His mother stopped, gathered her breath and slid her hand over Shelby's. "I'm sorry, but you're not going to like what I have to say about your father."

"Nothing you can say will surprise me now," Shelby insisted.

Jewell made a small "you're wrong" sound.

"I understand why you had an affair with Whitt," Roy interrupted before Jewell could say anything else. "I was drinking too much back then. We'd had a backbreaking year with the cattle sales. And I damn sure wasn't giving you the attention I should have been giving you."

Now Jewell's hand went over his. "I didn't have an affair with Whitt. With anyone." She paused again. "But I didn't nip Whitt's advances in the bud, either. I let the flirting go on because, well, because I was stupid and vain to think that his flirting meant I was still a desirable woman and not just the mother of a houseful of kids.

"I'm sorry," Jewell added, looking at both Rayanne and Rosalie.

"Flirting?" Roy repeated. "That's all that happened?"

"That was the beginning of what happened." Jewell's breath broke, and it took her a moment to regain her composure. "I started hearing rumors that Whitt and I were having an affair, and I called to ask him to try to put a stop to them. He didn't. As far as I can tell, he fueled those rumors with gossip of his own. Gossip that I was leaving you for him."

Seth went through each word. Words that he'd believed right from the start. That his mother was innocent, not just of murder but also of cheating on her husband.

"Then, how the devil did your DNA get in the cabin?" Seth asked.

"I went out there to confront Whitt, to tell him that I wanted no part of the rumors and begged him to set the record straight…"

The tears came, and his mother's breath caught again.

"Whitt raped me," she said.

Seth staggered back a step, and it felt as if someone had put a vise around his lungs and heart. Jewell caught on to both Roy and him when they cursed and tried to move away.

"Just stay put and listen," Jewell insisted, sounding a little stronger than she had just moments earlier. "I fought Whitt, and yes, I did stab him with a hunting knife that he kept in the cabin. It wasn't enough to kill him, but he did lose a lot of blood."

"You should have come to me. You should have told me," Roy snapped.

Jewell didn't agree with that, but she kept her gaze on Roy. "I was going to the sheriff first so that Whitt could be arrested, but Whitt staggered out of the cabin after me. He said if you found out what'd happened, that you'd go after him."

"I would have," Roy assured her. His eyes were narrowed and dark.

She agreed with a nod. "And either you would have killed Whitt or he would have killed you."

Roy cursed. "That didn't matter! He needed to pay for what he did to you. He still does."

"Yes, but we would have paid more. Because I didn't want you dead for what I'd done."

"What you'd done?" Rayanne asked. "You think you deserved to be raped for flirting with a man?"

"No, but I didn't deserve to get off scot-free, and Roy didn't deserve to be put in a position like that."

Again, the silence came. Enough silence for Seth to be able to process what'd happened over the past few hours.

"I need to call Cooper and tell him what happened," Seth said. "The statute of limitations has passed on filing rape charges, but maybe he can charge Whitt with obstruction of justice."

"Call Cooper later," Jewell insisted. "For now, let me just have this time. Not just with all of you, but with the boys."

The boys—Cooper, Tucker and Colt—still might not be receptive to having their mom back. Even after what Whitt had done to her. Because the bottom line was that she'd still left them twenty-three years ago. Maybe they'd see the reason she had done that and welcome her back with open arms.

Maybe.

"Whitt lied," Seth said, looking at Shelby.

Shelby nodded. She squeezed her eyes shut a moment. "He said he was shot and knifed by an unknown attacker and that he fell into the creek. He claims he got amnesia from the blood loss."

Jewell eased back in the chair. "Maybe he was attacked. But when I left him at the cabin, there wasn't anyone else around. And there was no amnesia. He called me early the next morning and said he'd heard that I'd gone home to Roy. Whitt was furious and insisted that he wouldn't allow that to happen, that if he couldn't have me, then Roy couldn't, either."

Hell, each new thing just made this worse and worse. Hearing it was torture for Seth. No doubt for Shelby, too.

Rosalie and Rayanne weren't faring much better.

Rosalie was crying. Rayanne, despite being nine months pregnant, looked ready to blast Whitt to smithereens.

But it was Roy's response that was the hardest to take.

He just sat there staring down at his hands. No doubt wondering what he should have done to stop this from happening. Seth wished he could have been there to stop it, too. No way should Jewell have gone through this much.

And it still wasn't over.

Even if they couldn't get Whitt for rape, they had to do something to make sure he got some serious jail time.

"I knew Whitt wouldn't give up," Jewell added a moment later. "I knew he'd keep pressing until he got what he wanted, and what he wanted was for me not to be with my husband."

"And you were also certain that I wouldn't forgive you," Roy added. "Because I believed the lies. Believed you'd been sleeping with Whitt and that's why you wouldn't let me touch you. I didn't know it was because you'd been…"

But Roy couldn't even finish that.

"Whitt said I had only one way out," Jewell continued. "That I was to leave town. Leave Roy. And because I didn't believe I deserved Roy or my family, I finally agreed with him."

"You made a pact with him," Seth concluded. "If you left, then Whitt would keep what he did a secret."

And that made Whitt a sick piece of slime.

Jewell nodded. "I took the girls because they were so young. I know my sons will never forgive me for that."

Probably not.

But Seth saw this from a different angle. If Jewell had never left Roy and Sweetwater Springs, then she would have never met his father. She wouldn't have raised him and become his mother. Out of all her kids, he was the only one who hadn't gotten a raw deal.

"I love you," Seth told her. "And I'm sorry that Whitt's manipulation and lies cost you your family."

She swallowed hard. "I still have my family." Jewell stood to hug Rosalie, Rayanne and then Seth, but Roy bolted from his chair.

"Roy!" Jewell shouted.

"I just need some air," he grumbled and stormed out.

"I'll go after him," Rosalie insisted. And out of the group of people in the room, she was probably the only one who could manage to talk some sense into him. Especially since Jewell wasn't allowed to leave the area yet.

"I knew this would hit him hard," Jewell said under her breath.

"It's hit us all hard," Rayanne corrected. "Whitt destroyed you, his family and ours."

That truth extended to Shelby, as well. Here, just a few hours earlier, she'd learned her father had essentially abandoned her, and now she'd just heard he was a rapist.

Seth intended to *deal* with Whitt about that…

And so would Roy.

"Whitt's possibly out of jail by now," Seth said.

Jewell gasped and shook her head. "Blue said he'd been arrested."

"He was. But Cooper called earlier to say he was going to have to release him. Whitt lawyered up, and there weren't any serious charges that Cooper could file to hold him."

"Oh, God," Jewell mumbled.

Yeah, they might need a little divine help on this one.

"I'm going with you," Shelby insisted, hurrying after Seth.

Seth didn't want to take the time to make other arrangements for Shelby. Every second counted right now. Maybe if he hurried he wouldn't be too late to stop Roy from committing murder.

Chapter Eleven

This day already had been a string of night-mares, and Shelby was terrified that it would get even worse.

As furious as she was with her father—and *furious* wasn't nearly a strong enough word for it—she didn't want Roy to gun him down. Not only for her father's sake.

But also for Roy's.

If her father had raped Jewell as she'd claimed, then Whitt deserved to be tossed in jail for any and every charge that could be pinned on him. However, he didn't deserve to die, and Roy certainly didn't deserve to be arrested for murder.

Seth hurried through security with Shelby in tow, and when they reached the front of the building, they immediately spotted Rosalie. She was in the parking lot and was shouting out her father's name, but Roy wasn't anywhere in sight.

"He left," Rosalie said, snapping toward Seth. "Dad got in his truck and sped off."

Seth cursed. "Stay here with Rayanne and Mom," he told his sister. "I'll find him."

Shelby hoped they could find him in time to stop him.

"Roy has a gun?" Shelby asked the moment they were inside the cruiser they'd borrowed earlier.

"With the way our luck has been running, he'll have a dozen." Seth took out his phone and handed it to her. "Call Cooper. Tell him what happened and that we're on our way back to the sheriff's office."

Which was no doubt where Roy would go.

Because like Jewell, he thought Whitt was still there. And perhaps he was, but Shelby was betting he'd already been released.

"Cooper, we have a problem," Shelby said when he answered, and then filled him in. It didn't take long to get confirmation of what she'd already feared.

"My father just left the jail," she relayed to Seth. "If Cooper sees Roy, he'll restrain him. He's also having Colt and Tucker go out and look for him in case he goes elsewhere."

Of course, that put Cooper and his brothers in a bad position since they loved their father. Still, there weren't a lot of options here. And time was running out.

Thankfully, the sheriff's office was only a

short drive from the county jail, but with each passing moment, Shelby could feel the dread building inside her. Even though Seth was staying quiet, she figured he was feeling the same thing.

Mercy, they both had just had a lot dumped on them, but it still wasn't anywhere near what Jewell and Roy had to be feeling.

"I'm so sorry for what my father did to Jewell," Shelby said.

It seemed to take Seth a moment to get his jaw muscles relaxed enough so he could speak. "Thank you for believing her."

Oh, Shelby believed the woman, all right. There'd been too much emotion and truth in Jewell's expression and words. Plus, her father's reputation of chasing women made it even more plausible.

As a child she'd heard gossip about Whitt's obsession with Jewell. Even Carla had mentioned it, usually when she'd been in a drunken stupor. Of course, in those stupors Carla had always made Jewell out to be the bad guy. The temptress who'd lured Whitt away from his wife and family.

But Shelby definitely saw this in a different light now.

"Jewell shouldn't have blamed herself for any part of this," Shelby went on. "But then, she was between a rock and a hard place. All this time she knew my father was alive, knew that he could come back at any time and boast to Roy what'd happened."

"And Roy would have killed him," Seth finished for her.

That still might happen.

However, there was a small silver lining to this. "Maybe now that the truth is out it'll help mend Jewell's relationship with her other sons. With Roy, too."

"Maybe." But it didn't sound as if Seth was convinced. Maybe because if Roy did end up in jail for murder, then Cooper and the others would be upset that Jewell hadn't told the truth sooner when Whitt was still missing.

And that brought Shelby back to something that had been troubling her since she'd heard what her father had said.

"Why would my father come back now? As much as he wanted Jewell to suffer because she rejected him, I can't believe he'd come back to Sweetwater Springs just to save her."

"No," Seth agreed. He paused a moment. "Maybe he came back because of the attacks against you."

That gave Shelby something else to think about. The attacks had been in the news, so it was highly likely that Whitt knew that someone had tried to kill Seth and her. Was that why he'd returned, to save her?

Part of her desperately wanted to believe that because it allowed her to hang on to the image she had of the father she'd lost when she was a child. But there was a flip side to considering something like that.

Did her father know *who* was trying to kill her?

Shelby didn't have time to dwell on the question, because Seth brought the cruiser to a stop directly in front of the sheriff's office. The moment Seth turned off the engine, the front door opened, and Cooper stuck out his head.

"My father's still not here," Cooper said immediately. "I think he might have seen Whitt driving away and followed him."

"Any idea where Whitt was going?" Seth asked.

"Home," Shelby answered, and Cooper verified that with a nod.

She wanted to kick herself for not thinking of it sooner. Certainly, Whitt would go to the ranch, and Roy would know that.

"I'll wait here just in case we're wrong and Roy and Whitt come back," Cooper said. "Head out to the Braddock ranch, and I'll call my brothers to get them out there, too."

Seth didn't waste even a second getting them headed in that direction.

"Who'll be at the ranch?" Seth asked her.

"Just the hands, the cook and maybe several housekeepers. My mother will be back at the mental hospital. Aiden and Laine are rarely there these days."

Of course, the hands and help could be hurt if Roy and her father got into a gunfight. Since she didn't know exactly where Tucker and Colt were, it could be up to Seth and her to try to stop this nightmare from happening.

Her family's ranch was just minutes from town and there was little traffic to slow Seth down. He took the farm road toward the property, but they were still a good mile from the main house when Shelby spotted the vehicles.

Three of them.

One she recognized as the black car her father had used to get to the sheriff's office. Another was Roy's truck. The third belonged to Annette. Her father's car and Roy's truck were still in the middle of the road, but Annette had pulled beneath some trees.

"You have to stop him!" Annette shouted the moment Seth stepped from the cruiser.

Seth didn't respond to Annette, but he drew his gun. "Stay inside the car," he warned Shelby.

She did. Mainly because she didn't want to do

something that would cause Seth to lose focus, but that would change if she could do anything to defuse this. Not that she had any influence with her father, but she'd have to try.

Shelby craned her neck so she could see around Roy's truck, and she quickly realized that things had already gone from bad to worse.

Roy was standing in the road, her father kneeling at his feet, and Roy had his gun jammed to the back of Whitt's head.

OH, MAN. THIS was not how Seth wanted things to play out.

"Roy, you need to put down that gun," Seth told him.

As expected, Roy didn't listen. In fact, he didn't even look at Seth. He kept his attention—and his gun—nailed to Whitt.

"He's going to kill Whitt," Annette cried out.

When Annette started to come closer, Seth motioned for Shelby to pull the woman back. He hated bringing Shelby into this. Hated that she even had to get out of the car, but if Annette physically tried to break up this fight, then someone was going to end up getting killed.

"Let Seth handle this," Shelby told her, and she wrestled Annette closer to the cruiser.

Seth turned his attention back to Roy. As expected, the rage was visible right there in Roy's face and muscles. His neck was corded and his mouth was tight, exposing his teeth.

"Roy, you can't do this." Seth tried to keep his voice level. With his own gun ready and drawn, he inched closer to the men.

The last thing he wanted to do was shoot Roy, but sadly it might come down to that. Seth silently cursed the badge he wore. It would be justice for Roy to kill the man who'd raped his wife, but Seth couldn't let Roy take the law into his own hands.

Not even under these circumstances.

"I can do this," Roy insisted. No level voice for him. Every ounce of his anger came through in those words. "If the law won't make him pay because of the statute of limitations, then I'll do what the law can't."

Whitt looked up at Seth. "You need to make Roy understand that Jewell just told him a whopper." Unlike Roy, there was no rage. Whitt didn't exactly look comfortable with a gun to his head, but he wasn't sweating, either. Maybe because he believed Roy wouldn't actually kill him.

Seth wasn't so sure.

Roy had been pushed to the edge, and men on the edge did all sorts of things they wouldn't do normally.

"And why would Jewell lie?" Seth asked, moving another step closer.

"To save face, that's why," Whitt readily answered. "To salvage her relationship with Roy."

"Roy and Jewell are divorced. As far as I can tell, she hasn't tried to salvage anything with him."

Whitt smiled. Not from humor. Now, here was proof of his own rage. "Then, you don't know Jewell. Roy managed to cast some kind of spell over her, and she could never see that he was no good for her."

Roy jammed the gun even harder against Whitt's head. "You raped my wife, and you're gonna pay for that."

"He didn't rape her!" Annette shouted. "Jewell's a liar. And worse. She's probably the one who had Marcel and those other people killed."

The woman tried to come closer again, but thankfully Shelby held her back. Seth also heard a welcome sound.

Sirens.

That meant one or more of Roy's sons were on the way. Good. Because they had a much better chance of defusing this than Seth did. That also meant he needed to keep Roy talking until backup arrived.

"Whitt will be arrested," Seth reminded him. "He obstructed justice, and there could be other charges from his faked death."

"I won't spend a day in jail," Whitt spat out.

"Especially not for any lies that Jewell told you. And I have proof she lied. I did nearly die. Someone attacked me, and it was Jewell. She told you all that stuff just to cover her guilt. Well, it won't work. She'll be the one who pays."

That didn't sound like an idle threat, but since Seth knew Jewell wouldn't lie about something like that, it might mean Whitt had something else shady up his sleeve.

"What proof?" Seth demanded.

Whitt smiled again. Not really a good idea, because Roy gave a fierce groan, and Seth could see the man fighting with himself over whether or not to pull the trigger. Seth hoped that was a battle that Roy would win.

"I have a letter," Whitt continued. "I sent it to Jewell twenty-three years ago and told her I wanted to break off our affair and reconcile with Carla. Jewell brought the letter to the cabin that day. She was upset. Crying. Begging me to stay with her. It has her prints on it."

"There was no affair!" Roy shouted.

The sirens were getting closer, but Seth wasn't sure they would arrive in time, so he maneuvered himself nearer to the men.

"A letter?" Seth challenged. "How would you have managed to hang on to that? You said someone stabbed and shot you and then you fell in the creek."

"I hid the letter before I was attacked. And I'm not gonna tell you where it's hidden because I don't want to give you the chance to destroy it."

Seth tried to figure out how this whole letter thing had actually played out. Maybe Whitt had written a letter all those years ago to set up Jewell. Maybe he'd set up his own attack, too, so he could disappear and start a new life. It wouldn't have been that hard to get Jewell's prints on some paper, especially since she'd indeed been at the cabin that day.

"What about Shelby?" Seth asked Whitt. This wasn't exactly the best time to get answers from Whitt, but maybe it would hook Roy's attention and give him second thoughts about pulling the trigger. "Are the attacks on her connected to you?"

No smile this time. But Whitt's eyes narrowed. "No. And don't you dare accuse me of trying to hurt one of my kids."

"You already did hurt us," Shelby said. "By walking out and letting us believe you'd been murdered."

"I know." Whitt dodged her gaze and shook his head. "It wouldn't have happened if I hadn't been attacked and gotten amnesia."

That didn't absolve him since he'd confessed that he'd had his memory back for a while now. One glance at Shelby and Seth could see that this was tearing her apart all over again. He needed to get her out of this situation now.

Thankfully, the cruiser pulled to a stop, and Cooper barreled out. He, too, had his gun drawn, but when he spotted his father, he lowered his weapon.

"Dad, this has to stop," Cooper insisted, not sounding like the sheriff but a very concerned son.

"You don't know what he did to your mother," Roy snapped. There were tears in his eyes now, and his hands were shaking.

"I do know what happened. Rosalie and Shelby called me after you ran out of the jail." Cooper didn't just lower his gun. He holstered it and walked past Seth to move closer to his father. "Whitt will pay. I swear, he will. But he can't pay like this, because you'll pay right along with him."

Roy made a strangled, hoarse sound. "But he raped her. He took her away from us."

"I know, but you've got to look beyond this moment. Jewell's already out of jail and is headed…home."

Seth figured that last word stuck in Cooper's throat. He wasn't exactly on good terms with Jewell. Of course, that had been before he'd learned the truth. Maybe now they could all start mending the damage Whitt had caused.

"You really want Jewell's first day of freedom to be at the jail waiting while I process you for murdering this lying dirtbag?" Cooper asked.

There. Seth finally saw what he'd been waiting for. Roy's surrender. It started in the man's eyes. Then his shoulders slumped before he backed away from Whitt.

Cooper moved in fast to take hold of his father's arm. And his gun. Cooper also maneuvered Roy several yards away from Whitt, and Whitt got to his feet.

"I'm filing charges, of course," Whitt said. Damn, it was not a good time for him to give Roy a smug look, because Cooper had to hold Roy back again.

Annette hurried to Whitt's side, but he didn't even acknowledge her. Instead, Whitt's attention went to Shelby.

"You're choosing the McKinnons and Seth Calder over me?" Whitt asked her.

The question alone no doubt hurt her, and coupled with the rest of this nightmarish day, Seth wasn't surprised that Shelby's first reaction was a slight hitch in her breath.

"Yes," Shelby answered.

Whitt looked as if he wanted to lash out at her for that, but he only shook his head. "I expected better from you. From all my kids. But I come back from the dead and find all of you in bed with my enemies."

"Enemies of your own making," Seth quickly reminded him.

The glare Whitt gave him was hard and long, but Seth matched it.

"Come on," Cooper said, ending the glaring match. "Dad, you ride with Seth, and I'll take in Whitt. I need statements from everyone." He glanced at Annette. "Including you. Follow us back to my office."

Annette cursed him, huffed, but she did head toward her car. However, she'd barely made it a step when Seth heard something. Some movement in the line of trees to his left.

A rustling sound.

But the sound was his only warning. A split second later, a shot blasted through the air.

Chapter Twelve

Shelby barely had time to register what was happening. Everything came at her too fast. And too loud.

Seth hooked his arm around her and pulled her to the ground. Again. Just as he'd done at the jail. It wasn't a second too soon because the next bullet slammed into the ground where she'd just been standing.

The fear returned, twisting and coiling inside her. But the anger came back, too. The outrage that rippled over her and caused her chest to tighten. So tight she could barely catch her breath. Could barely move. However, that didn't stop the nightmare from going through her head.

This couldn't be happening.

But it was.

Here, Seth and she were in danger yet again, and this time they weren't alone. Cooper, Roy, Annette and even her father were out in the open with bullets flying. Any one of them could be hurt or killed, and while she wasn't feeling fond of her father just now, she didn't want anyone else to die. Especially not at the hands of someone who was gunning for her.

Seth soon did something about that being-out-in-the-open part. He caught on to her and pulled her to the side of the cruiser. Again, barely in time because the shooter fired another shot.

At her.

Shelby couldn't see their attacker, didn't know exactly where he or she was, but there was no mistaking from the direction the bullets were taking that she was the target.

"Get down!" Cooper shouted. As Seth had done to her, he got Roy off the road and behind the truck that Roy had driven to the Braddock ranch.

Whitt and Annette ran, too, both taking cover at the back of her car.

"This is all your fault!" Annette screamed, and she just kept screaming.

Even though Shelby no longer could see the woman, she was pretty sure that Annette had meant the remark for her. And in a way it was her fault. There'd been one attack right after the other.

The murders.

The attempt to blow Seth and her to smithereens with that bomb.

She was at the center of that, and she should have realized that wherever she went, the danger would just follow.

Even here to her family's home.

The ranch hands would no doubt hear the shots and come running. Which could turn out to be a fatal mistake. Ditto for either of Cooper's brothers, who were likely on their way.

"Seth, can you see the shooter?" Cooper shouted.

Seth lifted his head, his attention zooming to the cluster of trees fifty yards from the road. Shelby had played in that area plenty of times as a kid and knew the trees extended all the way to a dirt road that was used to haul in hay.

If the gunman was there, then he was well hidden. And worse, he would have an easy escape route once he'd finished the job that he'd come here to do.

"I don't see him," Seth answered. "But I think he's using a rifle."

Shelby wasn't a firearms expert, but she figured that meant the shooter could be firing from a long distance. Maybe even beyond the trees.

"I need you to crawl toward the cruiser door," Seth told her. "It's bullet resistant, and you'll be safer there."

Shelby glanced back at the driver's-side door and nodded. "But you'll come with me."

Seth only shook his head. "I'll have a better vantage point from here."

"Not a safer one, though," she quickly pointed out.

Seth played dirty and brushed a quick kiss on her mouth. "Just get in the cruiser. This idiot wants to shoot you, and the best way to stop him is to get you in that car and out of his line of fire."

Since this was a bad time for an argument, Shelby did as Seth demanded. Without lifting her head, she began to make her way to the door. Cooper's cruiser was parked about fifteen yards away, and she could see Roy doing the same thing she was doing.

Cooper's orders, no doubt.

Seth and Cooper were trying to protect Roy and her. Maybe her father was trying to do the same for Annette, because Shelby no longer heard the woman's screaming. Or maybe Annette had realized she wasn't the one in danger.

More bullets came, each slamming into the cruiser. Shelby was shaking now. An adrenaline overload, no doubt, but she managed to get the door open, and she crawled inside.

"Stay down!" Seth warned her.

She did as much as she could, but Shelby stretched out across the seat so she could check the glove compartment for a gun. There wasn't one. Not that she could have risked opening the window or door to fire, but she would have preferred to be armed in case things got worse than they already were.

The shots kept coming.

Most of them hit the body of the car, but some went into the windows, cracking and webbing the glass. It was impossible for her to see outside, but at least the shots were still coming at her and not the others.

The radio on the dash made a static sound, and a moment later, she heard Colt's voice. "What the hell is going on?" he demanded.

"It's me, Shelby. A gunman attacked us at my family's ranch. I think Cooper and your father are okay."

Colt cursed. "Cooper's not answering his phone."

"Because the gunman has him pinned down. But I'm pretty sure he got your father inside the cruiser, where he'll be safe."

She hoped.

"Where's the shooter?" Colt asked.

"Somewhere in the trees on the south side of the road that leads to the main house."

More profanity from Colt. "What about Hance? Is he there, too?"

Shelby's heart skipped a beat. "I don't think so. Why?"

"Because I had a tail on him, and he was headed in the direction of your family's ranch. The tail lost him about a half hour ago."

That was more than enough time for Hance to have come to the ranch and gotten in position to launch this attack. Of course, Hance could have just hired someone to do the job, too.

"There's no sign of Hance," she assured Colt.

"Keep an eye out for him. There's no good reason for him to be in that area. Plenty of bad reasons, though."

Yes. And the bad reason could be murdering her.

"If you can, tell Cooper I'm less than a minute out," Colt said and ended the call.

Since Colt was an experienced deputy, he wouldn't just come driving into a hail of bullets, but maybe he could come up behind the gunman and capture him.

Shelby opened the driver's-side door a fraction, just enough so that she could call out to Seth and Cooper, "Colt will be here soon."

She tried to keep her voice as quiet as possible so she wouldn't alert the gunman as to what was happening, but she had to repeat it because of the deafening blasts drowning her out.

"Get back down!" Seth warned her.

She did, but the moment Shelby shut the door,

the shots stopped, and they went from the sounds of the blasts of the bullets to dead silence.

Did that mean the guy was reloading?

Or did hearing that the deputy was nearby cause him to run?

As much as Shelby hated not finding out who was shooting at them, at the moment she would settle for them all being safe. But soon she would need answers to stop this. She couldn't continue with this avalanche bearing down on her.

"He's at my two o'clock," Seth called out to Cooper.

Shelby lifted her head just enough so she could try to get a glimpse of him, but the sound of the bullet sent her right back down on the seat. It was just a single shot, and it didn't slam into the cruiser as the others had done.

But it slammed into *someone*.

She could hear Cooper groan in pain. Could hear Roy's profanity, too.

Oh, mercy.

Cooper had been shot.

That avalanche of emotions came. The fear and anger mixed with the guilt. Cooper was out here because of something her father had set in motion. Because some monster was after her.

There was another shot. Not from their attacker this time. But from Seth. He was no longer ducked down behind the car but was standing, his gun aimed in the direction of the gunman.

He fired again.

Shelby wanted to yell for him to get down, but at this point anything she said or did might distract him and make things worse. But she did pray.

"Did you get him?" someone shouted. It was Colt.

"I think I hit him in the shoulder," Seth answered, and in the same breath he looked back at Cooper. "How bad are you hurt?"

Shelby held her breath.

Waiting and praying.

"The bullet sliced across my arm," Cooper finally answered. "It's just a flesh wound."

"He's bleeding and needs stitches," Roy argued. "I've already called for an ambulance."

That didn't help the hard knot in her stomach. Cooper was the father of a young boy, and his wife was pregnant. They didn't need this. Not now, not ever. But maybe Cooper was right and it was just a flesh wound. Still, it must have looked more serious than that for Roy to have called an ambulance.

"When Tucker gets here tell him he's my backup," Colt snarled. "I'm going after this idiot who shot my brother."

"If you wait until Tucker arrives, he can stay with Shelby, and I'll go with you," Seth offered.

But Colt only waved him off and headed for the woods. Now she had someone else to worry about. Someone else who might be killed or hurt because of her.

Shelby opened the door again and spotted Cooper. He was indeed bleeding, and he had his right hand clamped over his left arm.

"Is there anything I can do?" she called out to him.

"Stay put," Cooper insisted.

"This guy might double back," Seth added.

Of course, she'd realized that was a possibility, but everything inside her was screaming for her to move. To do something.

"Is anyone else hurt?" Cooper asked.

"I'm okay," Shelby answered. Physically anyway. Inside was a different story.

"Fine," Seth piped in. "Annette and Whitt?"

In all the chaos, Shelby had forgotten about them. But she certainly thought of them now.

When neither answered.

"Whitt?" Seth tried one more time.

Still nothing, and after the way Annette had carried on earlier with the screaming, Shelby didn't think the woman's silence was a good thing.

"Everybody stay put," Seth insisted. "I'll check on them."

Shelby couldn't stop herself from sitting up, and she watched as Seth made his way to the back of the cruiser. He didn't call out to them any longer, and he kept his gun ready and aimed.

Each step he took caused Shelby's heart to beat even harder. So hard that she could feel the vibration of her pulse all over her skin. It didn't help her heartbeat when she heard Seth curse, but she couldn't see what'd caused that reaction.

"They're dead?" Cooper asked.

But Seth shook his head. "Not dead. Whitt and Annette are gone."

Chapter Thirteen

Seth finished his phone call and stared down at the blood on his shirt.

He cursed.

It wasn't his blood. It was Cooper's, but it shouldn't have been there. He already should have stopped the dangerous idiot who was causing all this trouble instead of letting one of his or her henchmen get to Cooper. Jewell already had enough to deal with—all of them did—without adding this.

"The medic said Cooper will be fine," he heard Shelby say. "They just needed to stitch him up."

Seth hadn't heard her come out of the bathroom at the McKinnon ranch guesthouse, and he'd been in such deep thought, he didn't even know how long she'd been in his bedroom doorway. However, he followed her gaze to the blood on his shirt. Blood he'd gotten on him when he'd helped Cooper get into his cruiser. Cooper had refused to ride in the ambulance, but Roy had assured everyone that he'd drive him straight to the hospital.

Mumbling another round of profanity at himself, Seth stripped off the shirt, tossed it in the laundry basket and looked in his closet.

Shelby walked in and sank onto the foot of the bed. She'd showered, no doubt to get the blood and grime off her, too, and she brought the smell of his soap into the room with her.

"You're running out of clean FBI clothes," she pointed out, glancing in his nearly bare closet.

Yeah, he was. He'd had bad days as an agent, but nothing like this. If he'd thought for one second that this fight was over, he would have put on his last clean suit, but a suit wasn't exactly the battle clothes he figured he'd end up needing.

Seth grabbed a black T-shirt instead and unzipped his pants, ready to replace them with some jeans. That was when he remembered Shelby was in the room. Not that he'd forgotten she was there exactly. Impossible to do that. But what he had forgotten was that some people were more modest than he was.

"I won't look," she said. She stared at the light switch. "I'd just rather stay put if you don't mind. Flashbacks," she added. "Bad ones."

He hated that she was having them, but would have been surprised if she hadn't been. It would take her a long time to stop remembering this nightmare they were living. Especially since they were still in the middle of it.

"I'm guessing you made some calls when I was in the shower. Did you find out anything?" she asked.

"Yeah." Nothing good, though, and he'd been on the phone almost the entire time not only during her shower but since they'd returned to the guesthouse. That was the reason he hadn't gotten around to changing his clothes. "Still no sign of the gunman, your father or Annette."

Shelby groaned, pushed her damp hair from her face. "How could my father have gotten far on a prosthetic leg?"

Seth didn't have an answer for that, and he wouldn't tell her that now that it was dark, the search had been called off until morning.

He ditched the black pants for the jeans and was still zipping up when Shelby turned and did something she'd said she wouldn't do. She looked at him.

Oh, man.

It wasn't one of the heated looks they'd been giving each other, but this one could be just as dangerous. Because her eyes were filled with tears. She quickly blinked them back, but Seth figured this was one battle she wasn't going to win.

He wouldn't win, either.

Seth had promised himself when he'd seen her in the doorway of his bedroom that he'd keep his hands off her. But those tears were a promise breaker. He sank down on the bed next to her and pulled her into his arms.

"Yes, I know we're playing with fire," she whispered.

However, she didn't back away. Muffling a sob, she dropped her head on his shoulder. "Except I guess a crying woman isn't much of a turn-on," Shelby added.

Not under normal circumstances, but this was Shelby, so the rules didn't exactly apply here. At least he had an out. He needed to go to the main house soon and check on his mother. After all, Roy and she had been divorced for years, and with the events of the day, Jewell's and Roy's emotions were running high.

But so were Shelby's.

And Jewell had a houseful of people to settle her in. Roy, Rosalie, Rayanne, Blue, Austin, Cooper's wife, and four grandchildren whom she would no doubt love getting to know. Shelby didn't have anyone but him at the moment.

Seth huffed. Yeah, it was thin logic since he could call Shelby's brother and sister, but the truth was Seth wanted to be the one to comfort her. He wanted *this*. Even though he was indeed playing with fire.

That was why he cursed when his phone rang. Then he cursed himself because this could be a critical update about the case, which should be his top priority. Solving this case would be a much better comfort to Shelby than leaning on his shoulder. His stomach clenched, though, when he didn't recognize the number on the screen.

"It's me, Whitt," the man said the moment Seth answered. "I need to talk to Shelby now."

Shelby was obviously close enough to hear her father's voice. "Where are you?" she demanded, after taking the phone from Seth and putting it on speaker.

"Someplace safe. For now anyway. I just wanted you to know that I didn't leave the scene voluntarily. Annette forced me at gunpoint to go with her. She led me through the woods and had a friend come and pick us up."

Shelby squeezed her eyes shut a moment. "Annette?" And yes, she sounded skeptical.

"The woman's crazy, and that's why I'm calling. You need to stay away from her. I managed to get away from her when she fell asleep, but I'm pretty sure she'll come looking for me."

"Where are you?" Seth repeated Shelby's question. "Where's Annette?"

"I left Annette at her ex-husband's hunting

cabin. If you dig, I'm sure you can find the location, and I hope you'll arrest her."

"I'd rather arrest you," Seth informed him. "Where? Are? You?"

Whitt hesitated. A long time. "Shelby, I love you." And with that the man ended the call.

The hang-up didn't exactly surprise Seth. Nothing about Whitt could at this point. But Seth would have preferred if the man had given them more about his whereabouts so they could find him and bring him in for questioning.

"Do you believe him?" Seth asked. He texted the number to an FBI friend and asked him to try to run a trace on it.

Shelby took a deep breath. "I'm not sure. I don't trust him, but I don't trust Annette, either."

Seth was right there with her on that. Of course, Annette and Whitt could be working together in all of this.

"Why did my father really come back?" Shelby asked. It sounded as if she was still trying to work it out in her head. "Jewell kept the secret of the rape all this time. Kept the secret about his being alive, too. And I find it hard to believe he would return just to save me. He could have hired someone to protect me without me even knowing it."

True, but this was something a father might do. *Might.*

"I don't think Whitt lied about loving you," Seth went on. "I believe he does. And maybe when he read about the attacks on you, he couldn't stop himself from coming back."

"Maybe." She paused. "But I did write that blog post, and maybe he was upset enough about that…"

There was no need for her to spell it out.

Seth remembered the threatening note: "You're a traitor, Shelby Braddock. And soon you'll be a dead one." Whitt might have wanted to punish her if he'd truly wanted Jewell convicted of his murder and was upset his daughter had even suggested her father's killer was still out there.

That was a big if.

Because if Whitt had wanted that, all he had to do was stay away and let everyone believe Jewell had murdered him.

His phone rang again, and this time it was a number Seth recognized. "Rosalie," he said after answering it. "Is everything okay?"

"Fine. Well, no danger anyway, but we're pretty sure Rayanne's in labor, so we're taking her to the hospital."

"*We?* Who's going with you?"

"Don't worry," Rosalie assured him. "Blue and Austin will be with us. Mom and Dad, too.

Plus, I called Cooper, and he said he'd wait with us at the hospital."

Since both Blue and Austin were lawmen, Seth relaxed a little. But that left him with another problem. "What about Cooper's wife, Laine, and the kids? I don't want them left without protection in case...well, just in case."

"I understand, and Austin's already working it out. Colt and Tucker will stay with the kids and the others at Colt's house and make sure everything's locked down. You and Shelby are more than welcome to go over there and join them, or you can come to the hospital with us. I'll warn you, though, it could be hours before Rayanne delivers."

"Hours," Seth repeated. "I don't want Shelby sitting in a public place for that long." Especially with Annette, Whitt and Hance out there. "And she'd probably be more comfortable here than at Colt's."

"I agree. I'll give you a call when the baby comes. In the meantime, Austin said he'll alert the ranch hands and they'll close the gate leading to the house after we leave for the hospital."

It wasn't a foolproof plan, since their attackers could get through some of the fences and make their way to the house. It also was possible someone could sneak in posing as a ranch hand or with the delivery trucks that came to the ranch several times a week. The McKinnon ranch could be a beehive of activity.

Still, staying put was safer than sitting in a hospital waiting room. Besides, he'd locked all the windows and doors and had set the security system. The ranch hands also would be armed, and with so many lawmen living on the grounds, they'd dealt with trouble before.

Seth hoped that trouble didn't continue tonight.

"Stay safe," Seth added. "And tell Rayanne I love her."

Seth was about to put away his phone when a text came in. It was from FBI agent Sawyer Ryland, and like just about every other message and call Seth had gotten about this case, this one wasn't good news, either.

"Your father was using a burner cell phone," Seth relayed to Shelby. "No way to trace it."

A burner could mean two things. Either Whitt was intentionally trying to conceal his location or else that particular phone was the only one he had access to. After all, Whitt's car had been left on the road at the Braddock ranch, so maybe his actual phone was in there. It was yet something else that Seth needed to verify.

And later, he would.

For now, though, he pulled Shelby to her feet so he could take her into the kitchen and get her something to eat. At least, that was the plan, but Shelby didn't budge.

"I'm so sorry I got you into this mess," she said.

Oh, man. They were back to that. "You didn't get me into anything. The person trying to kill you is responsible for that. And don't second-guess yourself about the article you wrote, your history with Hance or anything else."

Her forehead bunched up. "I hear the V-word in there somewhere. As in *victim*." She groaned, stepped away from him. "I really don't want to be one."

Neither did Seth, and he was about to tell her that when she whirled back around to face him.

"I don't want to be scared anymore," Shelby added. "And I don't want to keep hiding. I want to just go outside and demand a face-to-face with whatever idiot is behind this."

Seth had seen hard emotions in her eyes before, but this was a storm of a different kind. A storm that he was going to have to stop before Shelby made up her mind to do something stupid.

So he leaned in and kissed her.

A smart man would have come up with something a whole lot better, but Seth suddenly wasn't feeling very smart. Heck, maybe he just wanted to kiss her. And it seemed to work. Shelby stopped talking about a deadly showdown and slipped right into his arms.

It obviously wasn't the first time Seth had kissed her, but like the other times he felt that kick of surprise. Surprise that anyone could taste this good. Or feel this way in his arms.

Yeah, stupid.

Because kissing Shelby wasn't doing a thing to help them out of their dangerous situation.

His body didn't seem to care about that. And after the kissing had gone on for too long, the rest of Seth didn't care, either.

"You know this is a bad idea, right?" he asked as he shoved up her shirt and moved the kisses to the tops of her breasts.

"It's a terrible idea," she agreed. Though she did add a silky little moan to her agreement that pretty much told him this was going to happen whether it was bad or not.

Seth gave it one last-ditch effort and steeled himself to move away from her. But she didn't do that. Shelby slid her hand around the back of his neck, anchoring him in place.

With his mouth hovering over hers.

Could he have still stopped?

You bet.

Did he want to?

Not a chance.

The hovering vanished, and Seth kissed

Shelby again, knowing exactly where this kiss would take them.

SHELBY FIGURED THAT even though they'd just gotten started, Seth already had plenty of regrets about doing this. She probably should, too. But she didn't. It wasn't just her life that'd been turned upside down during the past two days.

So had her heart.

And her heart was telling her there was no place she wanted to be other than in Seth's arms.

Shelby just went for it. Thankfully, Seth did his part and cooperated. Or rather he continued to cooperate by kissing her until she was surprised she hadn't turned into a pile of ashes.

He was certainly good at this.

He'd had plenty of practice, no doubt. Because even now with the fire burning inside her, she still took the time to savor that drop-dead hot face.

And equally hot body.

She got a nice jolt of more heat when she stripped off his T-shirt and saw his perfectly toned chest that had been fueling a fantasy or two for her. Shelby kissed him there. On his stomach, too, and felt a wicked ripple of pleasure when his muscles tightened and reacted to her mouth.

"This would be a good time for us to come to

our senses," Seth said. But in the same breath, he stripped off her top and pushed down her bra.

"Yes, it probably would be a good time. *If* I wanted to come to my senses, that is. I don't."

Shelby especially didn't want good sense when Seth kissed her breasts. Yes, he knew what he was doing.

They pressed against each other. Body to body. So close that she took in his scent. Very nice. And she picked up the rhythm of his breathing.

Too fast.

Everything was moving too fast. There was no way to latch on to this kind of fire and hold on to it for long. Maybe, just maybe it would burn so hot that it would ease her need for him. But at the moment that didn't seem very likely.

Seth unzipped her jeans, pushed them off her. While fighting with her clothes, they tumbled onto the bed together. The kisses continued. Fast and frenzied. But somehow with all that frenzy Seth's touch managed to stay gentle.

Unlike hers.

Shelby felt all thumbs when she fumbled with his jeans. In part because her hands were trembling. In fact, her whole body was trembling.

Seth didn't help with his jeans. Instead, he went after her bra and panties, removing them with what seemed to be little effort while he continued to kiss the breath right out of her.

It didn't take long for her to realize she was stark naked and he wasn't. Her body put up a huge protest about that because more than anything she wanted him naked and making love to her.

Seth cooperated with that part, too.

"I want your jeans off now," she insisted.

He paused the touching and kissing just long enough to pull off his jeans and take a condom from his nightstand drawer.

"No," he said.

And it took Shelby a moment to realize the reason he'd said that was because she'd stopped trembling and had gone a little stiff. Not only that, her attention wasn't on his hot, naked body but rather the condom.

"You're the only woman I've had here," he said as if reading her mind.

She believed him, but even if she hadn't, that wouldn't have stopped her. Maybe that made her a fool. Another conquest in Seth's bed. But at the moment she was willing to take the risk that this could be a whole lot more.

That sent her arms around him.

The kisses and touches returned with a vengeance. No more gentleness, and Shelby was thankful for that. Right now the only thing she wanted was to finish what Seth and she had started.

Seth clearly wanted the same thing, because the moment he had on the condom, he pushed himself inside her. The blood rushed to her head. To other parts of her as well, and Shelby couldn't manage more than a moan of pure pleasure.

Oh, yes. Seth was very good at this.

He made love with the same intensity he did everything else in life. He took hold of her hands, gripped them in his. His gaze locked with hers while he slid, hot, into her.

It was perfect.

Well, except for the part about this not being able to last.

Her body was already begging for release, and Seth was more than willing to help her with that. He moved faster, harder, working that same magic as he had with his kisses. Except this was a kiss times a million.

Since she wasn't sure if she'd ever get to have this with him again, Shelby tried to hang on. She tried to savor every second. Every thrust. But she felt herself slip toward the edge.

And Seth quickly took her right over that edge and finished her.

Shelby could only hang on. Could only catch a glimpse of that incredible face before her vision blurred and the pleasure closed in around her. But she didn't need to see his face to realize something she didn't especially want to know.

Or feel.

She was falling in love with him.

Chapter Fourteen

Seth stood at the kitchen window of the guest-house, sipping his coffee and trying to figure out just how badly he'd messed up.

He was guessing pretty badly.

Not the sex. That'd been the opposite of bad. Right up there on the top of the list of things that'd felt darn good. Still, that didn't mean *good* wouldn't make things worse than they already were.

As an FBI agent he'd had it drilled into him not to get personally involved with an investigation.

Well, this was as personal as it got.

He only hoped it wouldn't come back to bite him.

Seth topped off his coffee and went to check on Shelby. She was still in his bed. Asleep and naked. Exactly the way he'd left her nearly an hour ago. Face down, hair a beautiful mess against the stark white pillow. The sheets were coiled around her as if she'd been fighting a fierce battle with them.

Or rather fighting with the nightmares.

She'd had a couple of them during the night. Bad ones. Seth had held her, but kisses weren't going to put an end to this. What he needed was a break in the case. If they could just find Annette, Whitt or the shooter, he might get some answers. But all were still missing.

He had just made his way back to the kitchen to check his emails on the laptop he'd left on the table when he heard the sound of a car engine. His body went on instant alert, but he soon saw the familiar truck pull to a stop next to the main house.

It was Roy and his mother, both looking as tired as Seth felt.

Jewell stepped out, her attention going straight to the window. She waved when she spotted Seth, said something to Roy, who headed for the main house. Jewell started walking toward the guesthouse.

Oh, man.

Normally, he would have enjoyed seeing his mother, especially now that they didn't have to visit behind the Plexiglas at the jail, but he wasn't especially eager for her to learn that Shelby and he had shared a bed. Still, he couldn't ask Jewell to stand out on the small back porch and talk.

Not with a gunman still out there who could target her with a rifle. So Seth quickly shut his bedroom door, turned off the security system and hurried back to the kitchen to let Jewell in.

His mother managed a smile. A genuine one from the look of it. But he saw the fatigue in her eyes now that they were face-to-face.

"There's no baby yet," she explained. "Rayanne's labor stopped shortly after midnight, so she's resting now. But the doctor's keeping her because if the contractions don't start up again on their own, he's going to induce."

"Induce?" Seth asked, but he waved off the question. It didn't seem like something he wanted to know, and he hated that his sister had to go through this.

"Rayanne will be fine," Jewell assured him. That sounded genuine, too. Good. One less thing for him to worry about. "Roy and I are here just for a change of clothes and to freshen up, and then we'll head back."

"I'm sure Rayanne will appreciate that," he replied. "You want some coffee?"

Jewell nodded and sank down at the kitchen table as he poured her a cup. "Did Shelby and you have a…rough night?" she asked.

The question seemed innocent enough, but his mother had a sixth sense when it came to her kids.

"Yeah, it was a little rough," he settled for saying. "Probably a lot better than yours, though. Your first night out of jail in months, and you ended up sleeping in a hospital room."

"It was still a good night."

Seth knew something about that, too, since that was the kind of night he'd had. Good mixed with bad. He also knew Jewell wouldn't have wanted to be anywhere other than with Rayanne while she was going through this.

His mother glanced around the place. Not that it took too much glancing to see most of it. "I'd forgotten how little room there is here. When will you be moving to the new house?"

"Soon." He hoped. "I've got the keys to the place. Already hired the ranch hands. But I haven't had time to look for livestock or furniture yet."

Their conversation seemed a little too much like small talk considering several thousand-pound elephants were in the room.

"How are things with Roy?" Seth asked, sitting down next to her at the table.

No genuine smile this time, though she did attempt one. One no doubt meant to reassure him. But as her son, he had a sixth sense about her, as well. So Seth kept staring at her to let her know he expected a real answer.

"It's complicated." A heavy sigh left her

mouth. She slid her hand over his, gave it a comforting pat. "I don't expect him just to forgive me for abandoning him and the boys."

Well, Seth sure expected it. "You didn't abandon them. You did what you thought was necessary to save Roy's life."

"Maybe." She drew back her hand and stared down into her coffee.

"Maybe?" he questioned.

"It was partly selfish, too. Leaving meant I didn't have to deal with Whitt. It meant shoving all the hate and anger so deep that I didn't have to feel it." She paused. "Of course, I'll have to deal with it now. All of you will. That's why I've decided to forgive Whitt."

Seth was glad he was seated, because that gave him a jolt. "He doesn't deserve your forgiveness."

He would have added more to his argument, but he heard footsteps.

Shelby's.

They were coming from the bedroom, and Seth held his breath, hoping she wouldn't come into the room bare butted. Thankfully, she was dressed.

"I'm sorry. I didn't mean to interrupt," she said when her gaze landed on Jewell. She turned to walk away.

"You didn't interrupt," Jewell assured her, and

she got to her feet. "Stay, please. I need to be getting back to the main house anyway. After a shower and a bite to eat, Roy and I are going back to the hospital so we'll be there when Rayanne has the baby."

"Seth's right. You don't have to forgive my father," Shelby blurted out. "He doesn't deserve it." Obviously, she'd heard at least part of the conversation he'd had with his mother. "I'm not sure I could forgive him if I were in your place."

With that soft half smile on her face, Jewell went to her and pulled Shelby into her arms for a brief hug. "I'm not doing it for Whitt. I'm doing it for me. It's the only way I can get on with my life."

Heck, that was too much logic considering that Seth was still seeing red over what Whitt had done to her. And he always would. One way or the other, Whitt would pay. Not just for the rape, but for what he'd done to Shelby and the rest of her family.

He stood and watched Jewell make her way back to the main house. Roy was waiting for her on the porch and even opened the door for her.

"Roy and Jewell are getting back together?" Shelby asked, watching, as well.

Seth had to shrug. "Hard to say. I know they got in touch with each other after Rosalie's daughter was kidnapped over a year ago. They were trying to help her find the baby, and I think maybe that brought them a little closer."

It'd broken the ice between them anyway, and thankfully, it'd had a happy ending with Rosalie's daughter being found. Now both his sisters were making homes at the ranch. Colt, Tucker and Cooper, too.

Leaving Roy and Jewell alone in that big ranch house.

If any fire was left between them, being under the same roof would certainly fuel it.

As Seth had learned with Shelby.

"Is everything okay?" she added.

It took him a moment to realize she was no longer looking at Jewell and Roy but at him.

"Fine." And because he thought they both could use it, he brushed a kiss on her cheek. Then her mouth. "You?"

"Better now." Shelby's smile didn't last long. "Anything new about the investigation?"

That was his cue to get down to business. "Nothing, but I need to check in with Colt anyway."

He reached for his phone, but reaching was as far as Seth got before he heard a sound he didn't want to hear.

His mother screamed.

JEWELL'S SCREAM SLICED through Shelby like a knife.

Sweet heaven.

What'd happened now?

"Stay behind me," Seth said, throwing open the door. "What's wrong?" he shouted.

No answer. That caused the skin on the back of her neck, to crawl and Shelby's thoughts jerked back to another time, another place. Another attack.

"Mom?" Seth tried again.

When he didn't get an immediate answer, he went outside, but then glanced back at her. Shelby saw the debate going on in his head. If he left her alone that could be dangerous, exactly what their attacker would want him to do. But his mother was clearly in trouble.

"Keep low and hurry," Seth finally said. Before he'd even finished they started running toward the main house.

They were barely halfway there when she spotted Roy coming out of the backyard. "It's okay," he said. "It's not real."

Shelby couldn't imagine what Roy meant by that, and it only made Seth run even faster.

As soon as they reached the porch she saw Jewell, but because of the steps and posts, she couldn't see what had taken the color right out of the woman's face.

"It's not real," Roy repeated, leading them up the steps. "Jewell, you need to get inside." When she didn't budge, Roy took her by the arm and led her to the kitchen.

The porch stretched all the way across the back of the house, and it was lined with white wicker chairs, plants and even a porch swing.

And beneath the swing was a body.

Shelby's heart jolted even though she kept reminding herself that Roy had said it wasn't real. But it certainly looked real, like the other bodies they'd discovered over the past couple of days.

This one had a mask, too.

Of Seth's face.

"Get inside," Seth told her and, as Roy had done, he maneuvered Shelby into the kitchen with his mother.

Jewell and she didn't go far, however. They stayed right in the doorway looking out while Seth and Roy went toward the "body."

"I didn't touch it, but if you look closer, you'll see it's not real. It's just clothes stuffed with mulch and straw from the flower beds," Roy explained. "It wasn't here last night when we went to the hospital."

A chill rippled through Shelby. This meant someone had gotten onto the ranch. The killer. Or else someone who worked for the killer.

Seth studied the body for only a few seconds

before his gaze whipped around the backyard and the rest of the property. A few ranch hands were out in the nearby pasture, but they didn't seem to alarm him or Roy. So they must have known the hands. And that meant there was no sign of the person who'd left that fake body. A fake that no doubt was designed to scare them.

It'd worked.

Shelby was scared.

It had been bad enough to see masks of her father and her own face, but now the killer was using Seth's image. Of course, she'd known Seth was likely a target right along with her, but it drilled the point home to see what the killer intended.

"How could the killer have gotten all the way to the house?" Shelby asked no one in particular.

Seth tipped his head to the fence on the far side of the large pasture. She'd remembered him saying that an attacker could get in that way. And he or she apparently had.

"I'll ask the hands if they saw anything," Roy volunteered.

"And I'll call Cooper to let him know," Seth added. "For now, though, I think we should all stay inside."

Seth was already moving Roy in that direction, but he took it a step further. Once they were all in the kitchen, he shut the door, locked it.

"You had the security system armed the whole time you were at the hospital?" Seth asked.

Roy nodded. "All the windows and doors are wired so if any of them had been opened or broken into, the alarm would have gone off, and the security company would have called us."

That gave Shelby a little relief. At least it probably meant someone wasn't inside the house, waiting to kill them.

Probably.

No doubt that slim hope was why Seth kept them in the kitchen, away from the windows, while he called Cooper to report the incident. Roy also made a call to one of the ranch hands, and he told him to ask around to see if anyone knew anything about the fake body.

"None of the ranch hands would do anything like this," Roy explained when he ended the call. "I trust them, and we haven't hired anyone new in months." He paused. "But someone could have cut through the pasture and made it to the porch. There aren't any security sensors back there."

Yes, and the person easily could have come on foot, carrying just the clothes and mask since they'd used the bedding cover to stuff the garments.

"We need to check the grounds," Seth insisted.

Roy nodded and made another call to one of

his ranch hands. He asked for a thorough search of every part of the grounds and the outbuildings. Roy also asked them to look for any tracks leading to the house. It hadn't rained in days, so maybe this monster had left footprints.

"The kids," Jewell said on a gasp. "They're at Colt's."

That prompted another call. This one from Seth to Colt. "Are you okay?" Seth immediately asked the deputy.

Since Seth didn't put the call on speaker, Shelby held her breath, waiting. Jewell did, too, and even clutched Shelby's hand.

"They're all right," Seth relayed to them several moments later when he finished the call. "Both Colt and Tucker are there with their wives, Cooper's wife and the kids. They're locked up and with the security system on. Colt's going to call the hospital and alert Blue and Austin."

Shelby didn't know either man very well, but since they were both lawmen, she hoped that would be enough protection for Rayanne and Rosalie.

"Cooper's on his way here?" Shelby asked.

Seth nodded. "But he wants to stop by Colt's first. He said to call if we spotted anyone or anything else suspicious."

Of course Cooper would want to see his wife and son to make sure they were all right. Shelby understood that. Especially since her sister, Laine, was also at Colt's. There'd been no indication that this killer would go after anyone else in the family, but that could change.

After all, the killer had made it all the way to their doorstep.

"I want to go through the house just in case," Seth said. "All of you should stay here."

Shelby stepped in front of him. Her first instinct was to stop him, but the truth was the place did need to be searched since someone could have jammed the security system and sneaked in.

"It'll be okay," Seth added, and he dropped a quick kiss on her mouth.

Since Jewell and Roy were standing right there, they saw the kiss. Probably knew what was going on between Seth and her, too. Which made Shelby give their relationship some thought as she watched Seth walk out of the kitchen.

Exactly what *was* going on between Seth and her?

Yes, they'd slept together, but it was entirely possible that when this ordeal was over, whatever this was between them would be over, too.

Not exactly something she wanted to consider.

Nor did she have time to give it another thought, because Roy's phone rang.

"It's Arlene, the horse trainer," Roy told them and answered the call.

Shelby couldn't hear what the woman said, but she could tell from the way Roy's face dropped that it wasn't good news. Seth must have seen it, too, when he hurried back into the kitchen.

"What's wrong?" Seth immediately asked Roy.

"One of the hands found a body near the back fence. A real body."

That took the air right out of her lungs. With all the other deaths, Shelby figured she should be semi-immune to that slam of adrenaline. But maybe a person never got immune to that.

Roy paused. "It's a man's body, but he's got a mask of Whitt on his face, so the hand can't tell who it is."

"Tell him not to touch the body or the mask," Seth insisted. "We might get lucky and there'll be some trace evidence. I'll get Cooper and a CSI team out here. Oh, and tell the ranch hand to come back toward the house. The killer could still be out there."

Oh, mercy. He was right.

"I'll call Cooper," Jewell volunteered, and she hurried to the house phone mounted on the wall over one of the counters.

While Roy finished his call, Shelby took hold

of Seth's arm as he moved toward the door. "You can't go out there," she said.

"I'm not, but I need to keep watch." Seth's gaze met hers. "It's possible the body is a ruse to get me out of the house and away from you."

Of course it could be. This idiot had tried everything else to kill them, and she didn't even know why.

"I'll reset the security system so the alarm will sound if anyone breaks in," Roy volunteered. "Then I'll make sure all the windows and doors are still locked."

"I'll go with him," Jewell insisted, and she took two guns from a cabinet over the top of the fridge. She handed one to Shelby and kept one for herself. "Maybe you won't have to use it," she added.

But the words had hardly left her mouth when Jewell froze. "Do you smell that?"

Shelby didn't. Not at first. But it didn't take her long to realize what had put that alarmed look in Jewell's eyes.

Smoke.

There was barely a trace of it in the air, but it was indeed there. And it didn't seem to be coming from anywhere in the kitchen. Nothing was on the stove or in the oven.

Seth must have smelled it, too, because he hurried to one of the windows, looked out.

Then he cursed. "Someone set fire to the porch."

Chapter Fifteen

Seth's first instincts were to hurry out onto the porch and try to stomp out those flames. He could see the fire snapping around, and it could spread to the rest of the house.

But the fire also could have been set to draw him outside.

Or maybe not.

After all, a gunman could have shot Shelby and him, Roy and Jewell, too, when they had been on the porch earlier.

So what was this fire all about?

He doubted it'd started by accident. In fact, there could have been some kind of incendiary device concealed inside the clothes. In hindsight, he should have given the fake body at least a cursory inspection, but he hadn't wanted to destroy any potential evidence. Even more, he'd wanted to get Shelby, Roy and Jewell inside.

Hell. The killer could have been out there that

whole time, watching them. Waiting for the perfect moment to strike.

Behind him he heard Shelby calling 9-1-1 to request a fire truck. He also heard Roy hurrying back into the kitchen.

"There's another fire on the front porch," Roy blurted out.

That was *not* what Seth wanted to hear.

He remembered the timer on the bomb at the jail. Had these fires been triggered by some kind of timer, as well?

It was the only thing that made sense.

That was because he'd been keeping watch out back and hadn't seen anyone set fire to the dummy. Not only that, with the ranch hands milling around, the killer probably wouldn't have risked being seen. The timers could have been set during the night when there was less chance of being caught.

Roy pulled a fire extinguisher from beneath the sink, but Seth stopped him when he rushed toward the door.

"It's a trap?" Roy asked.

"Could be."

A trap that might succeed if the fires overtook the house. One way or another, the killer could be forcing them outside.

Seth had another look at the back porch and yard. Two ranch hands were running toward the house. No doubt ready to help with the fires, but they also could get killed.

"Stay away from the windows and doors," Seth told Shelby and his mother. "I'll try to put out the fire on the back porch. Roy, disarm the security system and cover me."

Roy nodded, punched in the code on the keypad by the door. With his gun still in his right hand, Seth took the extinguisher in his left.

"But you could be shot," Shelby quickly pointed out.

Yeah, it was a real concern, but Seth tried not to let that concern show too much. "Roy will keep watch."

Shelby was still protesting when Seth hurried out on to the porch. "Take cover," he shouted out to the ranch hands. "A gunman could be out here."

Seth knew both men, Quint and Darnell, and they'd worked at the ranch the entire eight months he'd been there. The men ducked behind a detached garage.

"What do you want us to do?" Darnell asked.

"Work your way to the front porch and try to do something about that fire there. But be careful."

The men nodded, and, using the buildings and vehicles for cover, they started toward the front of the house.

Seth tried to keep watch, but it was hard to see through the billowing smoke. Hard to breathe, too, when the wind whipped that smoke right at him.

He aimed the extinguisher at the fire and started coating the area with the thick foam. It was a battle, however, that he was quickly losing. The flames were going out, but the smoke was getting worse.

"There's another fire," Quint shouted. "It's on the east side of the house, and it's already pretty bad."

Hell. And judging from the volume of smoke, there was probably a fourth fire on the west side. This piece of dirt was obviously trying hard to get them out of the house.

Seth's attention went to the vehicles. With the exception of Roy's truck, the others had been outside all night. The killer could have planted another bomb or device in any of them. And this time the timer might not fail. That meant he had to get Shelby, Jewell and Roy to the truck. There probably hadn't been enough time to plant something on it.

He went back in the kitchen, hoping this plan wouldn't turn out to be exactly what the killer wanted them to do. "Roy, we're leaving in your truck. Give me the keys and I'll move it right next to the porch."

Shelby opened her mouth, no doubt ready to tell him that was a bad idea. But it must have occurred to her that all that were left for them were bad ideas. Staying put could be fatal since they could be burned alive or die from smoke inhalation. At least this way they had a chance.

Seth took the keys, raced back onto the porch and jumped off near the truck. Quint had been right about the fire being bad on that side of the house. The flames were already eating their way to the second floor. It wouldn't be long before the fire department got there, but Seth wasn't sure they'd make it before the whole place was engulfed in flames.

Still keeping watch around him, Seth got in the truck and said a quick prayer before he turned the key in the ignition. No explosion. The engine started right off. Thank God.

He didn't waste a second. Seth sped to the porch and brought the truck to a stop directly in front of the steps. Too bad it was also directly in front of the thick white smoke. Coughing and trying to cover their mouths, Shelby, his mother and Roy came out of the kitchen.

Each step they took seemed to take an eternity, and Seth's heart stayed right there in his throat.

This had to work.

The three were so close. Already on the steps when the shot tore through the air.

No. Not this. Not now.

"Get down!" Seth shouted to them, and he turned to see who'd fired at them.

Because of the smoke, he couldn't see anyone, but he was certain it'd come from the west side of the house. Before that even had time to register in his head, another bullet slammed into the truck.

This one from the east side.

They were caught between two gunmen and two fires. Any of which could kill them if he didn't do something fast.

"Stay low, but try to get into the truck," Seth told them.

But the gunmen clearly weren't going to let them escape. More shots came at them. All from the west side. And all the shots went right into the truck engine. It didn't take long to do exactly what the shooter had set out to do.

Disable the truck.

Seth cursed and looked around for plan B. The garage was too far away, but the equipment barn was close enough.

Maybe.

It was also the place where a killer could be hiding, knowing that he or she had given them no other way out.

Another shot came. Not at the frenzied pace of the ones that'd been aimed at the engine. This one landed on the porch. Much too close to Shelby and the others.

"This way." Seth motioned for them to make their way to the truck. Yes, the engine was shot, but they could still use it for cover. "Crawl beneath it and then get into the barn. But I need to go in there first."

To check for a killer.

Once the three were beneath the truck, Seth barreled out the door and hurried into the barn. He stepped inside, gun ready, and he had to take a moment to let his eyes adjust to the darkness. A light switch was in the tack area, but that was yards away. Too risky for him to try to get there, especially since Shelby and the others were still outside.

Seth's gaze whipped from one side of the barn to the other. It wasn't as big as some of the others on the property, but this one was filled with tractors, mowers and other equipment.

Plenty of places for a killer to hide.

He wanted to check them all to make sure it was safe.

But he didn't get a chance to do that.

Outside, he heard some strange sounds. A sort of thud, as if something had hit the ground. It didn't take him long to figure out what exactly.

A tear gas canister.

And not just one of them but two, and they both started spewing the choking gas right around the truck.

SHELBY'S EYES AND throat were already burning from the smoke, but the cloud of tear gas made it a thousand times worse. Her breath just stopped, and with her chest pounding, it felt as if she was on the verge of a panic attack. Everything inside her was screaming for her to run and get away before she suffocated.

With a firm grip on her gun, Shelby scrambled out from beneath the truck with Roy and Jewell right behind her. Seth was in the barn entrance waiting for them, and the moment they were inside he pushed them behind the wheel of a giant tractor.

"Stay down," Seth warned through his own coughs, and he slid the barn door shut before he took cover behind another tractor.

There hadn't been much light in the place, and closing the door certainly didn't help. But it did keep out some of the tear gas and smoke.

Shelby held her hand over her mouth, hoping it would help, and she blinked hard to try to clear her eyes. She still couldn't see much of anything, but Seth apparently could. He turned, pivoting to all sides of the barn. No doubt to make sure no one was lurking inside, ready to kill them.

"Seth?" one of the ranch hands called out.

"In the barn," he managed to answer before the gunshots started again. It wasn't the barrage it'd been before, but it probably was enough bullets to keep any of the ranch hands from getting close to the barn.

Oh, mercy.

Did that mean the killer had set a firebomb in the barn, too? If so, he or she was planning to burn them alive. That nearly got Shelby bolting again, but then she heard the sirens in the distance. The fire department. Maybe they'd make it in time to stop whatever was about to happen.

Or not.

Because the next sound Shelby heard was a voice. Not Seth's or that of any of the ranch hands, but it was a voice she recognized.

"Come out so I can see you," the woman said.

It wasn't a shout. Her voice was as calm as if discussing the weather. But Shelby figured they finally knew the identity of the killer.

Annette.

But was Annette working alone? Or was Whitt in on this?

"Why are you here?" Seth asked her. "And where's Whitt?"

"I don't know where he is. And as for why I'm here, isn't it obvious?" Annette countered.

Shelby moved enough so she could peer around the tire, but all she could see was the shadowy figure on the side of some shelves. A moment later, a light came on. Still not very bright. It was a single exposed bulb dangling from the ceiling. But it was more than enough to verify that it was indeed Annette.

Armed.

And she had something strapped around her chest.

"Why don't you spell it out for me?" Seth insisted. "Tell me why you're here. And why you're wearing explosives."

Sweet heaven.

Both Jewell and Shelby gasped. Yes, they were explosives, all right. They looked to be sticks of dynamite lined up vertically and taped around her body.

Clearly, Annette had lost it, and there was no telling what she would do. This was something worse than a nightmare because now the danger wasn't to just Seth and her but to his mother and Roy, as well.

"I'm here to kill the traitor and the witch who lured Whitt away from me," Annette said. "Shelby shouldn't have written that stupid blog post, questioning Jewell's guilt. And Jewell never should have gone after Whitt in the first place. She has to die, too."

Shelby felt the punch of dread in her gut. Not dread for herself, but because she was the reason all of this had been happening. Of course, Jewell was no doubt feeling something similar even though she'd never *gone after* Shelby's father. That was all a figment of Annette's messed-up head.

"If you shoot me," Annette continued, her voice still calm, "I'll push the button and set off the explosives. The blast won't just kill us but anyone who's nearby."

Shelby saw the device in Annette's left hand. It looked like some kind of tube, but it probably was a trigger. One that the woman might be able to press if Seth did indeed shoot her.

"If you wanted Shelby and my mother dead, why didn't you just shoot us when we were on the porch?" Seth asked her.

"I didn't have everything in place yet. I do now."

"You mean your hired guns and the fires." Seth moved to the other side of the tractor, no doubt trying to get into position to do something about this.

But what?

"And the body by the fence," Annette readily admitted. "I needed to do something to lure some of the ranch hands away from the house, and I figured that body would do it. A nice little surprise for all of you."

Who had she killed this time? And the first answer that came to Shelby's mind was her father. After all, Whitt had said that Annette had forced him to leave the Braddock ranch at gunpoint.

Maybe the woman had carried that one step further.

Of course, it could be something even sicker than that if Annette had gone after someone in Jewell's family.

"Don't think your lawmen stepbrothers are coming to save you," Annette went on. "I've set up a roadblock. He has orders not to kill Cooper or the others, but he'll shoot out the engines the way he did to the truck and keep them pinned down. And those firemen won't come closer when they hear shots."

That was true, but Shelby hoped that none of Jewell's sons or the firefighters got hurt, or worse.

"How'd you even get in here?" Roy called out. No calmness in his voice. Pure anger.

"I sneaked in last night. I've been waiting ever since. I figured Shelby would be more likely to cooperate if others' lives were at stake. Like

Seth's and yours. Shelby and Jewell are the only ones I plan to kill."

"That's not gonna happen," Seth assured her. "You really want to get the death penalty for killing the woman you believe is an old rival and someone who wrote a blog post?"

"It wasn't just a blog post!" Annette shouted. "It was a betrayal by a traitor. For years I've worked to bring her father's killer to justice, and then she gave it all up when she looked at your pretty face."

"You're wrong," Shelby spoke up. "I wrote that post before Seth and I even got involved. And besides, I was right. Jewell didn't kill Whitt."

"That doesn't matter!" This shout was even louder than the last one. "All that matters is you're a traitor. You cut your daddy to the core when he read it."

Maybe. But Annette obviously was unstable, so there was no telling how much of this was truth and how much was fantasy.

"And as for the death penalty, that won't happen," Annette insisted. "Because I don't intend to stay around afterward. If Whitt can disappear for twenty-three years, then so can I. Now, enough of this talk. Shelby and Jewell, get out here now, or I press this button and we all die."

It was a risk, but Shelby figured she'd try to

distract the woman a little longer just in case Seth could defuse this situation. Plus, Shelby was banking on the fact that Annette truly didn't want this to be a suicide mission.

"So because I upset my father, you murdered at least five people?" Shelby asked. "And now you want to add Jewell and me to your list?"

"I didn't kill Marcel." Annette's voice broke, and a loud sob came from her mouth. She repeated it in a whispered tone that sounded as if she was genuinely grieving for the man. "I think Hance did that," she added, saying Hance's name like a profanity. "To punish you. And me. He knew killing Marcel would be personal."

Shelby couldn't discount that. After all, Hance had murdered his own wife. But then, Annette was a killer, too. She hadn't denied murdering the others, though.

She heard Roy's phone buzz. Maybe a text message. But Shelby couldn't see what popped up on the screen.

"I worked so hard to put Jewell away so that Whitt and I could have a life together," Annette went on. She was crying now. Sobbing, actually. Maybe the tears would distract her enough so that she wouldn't see Seth inching his way toward her.

"A life together?" Shelby questioned, hoping

the sound of her voice would cover Seth's movements. "What did you do, Annette? What?"

She shook her head. "Everything. I pressed the DA to bring charges against Jewell. And I'm the one who planted the bone fragments I took from Whitt's house. Randy Boutwell helped me."

Boutwell, the first dead man.

"Why'd you kill him if he helped you?" Shelby asked.

"Because he was blackmailing me, that's why. I killed Meredith because she was asking too many questions, and I didn't want her around to tempt Whitt. Women are always throwing themselves at Whitt," she added. "Plus, killing her was a good cover for Boutwell's murder. The cops would be focused on a serial killer and not specifically Boutwell."

That was partly true. Seth and the other lawmen certainly hadn't suspected that Boutwell was the original target.

"Now get out here!" Annette screamed. "And put down those guns."

Since Seth still wasn't in place yet, Shelby just kept pushing. Yes, it was a risk. Anything was at this point, but she had to try. She motioned for Jewell and Roy to get all the way onto the floor, but they both stayed put. In fact, Roy looked ready to jump at Annette.

"You're right about women always throwing themselves at my father," Shelby continued. "Is that why you shot him in the cabin twenty-three years ago?"

Annette froze, a strange look coming over her face. "That was an accident. I knew that he'd been with Jewell, and I got mad. So mad that I grabbed a gun and went inside to confront him. But the gun went off. I swear, I didn't pull the trigger on purpose."

Just talking about it seemed to put her in some kind of trance. Maybe because she couldn't deal with the fact that she had indeed nearly murdered the man she purportedly loved.

Or maybe Annette had now murdered him. And left his body as a distraction for the ranch hands.

Shelby didn't have time to dwell on that because she saw Seth move. Thankfully, Annette didn't seem to notice that he'd managed to get so close to her. Shelby didn't know exactly what he had in mind.

But she soon found out.

Seth came running from behind the tractor and launched himself at Annette.

Chapter Sixteen

Seth knew he had to do this fast, or they were all going to die.

He rammed into Annette, latching on to her left hand, which held the triggering device for the explosives. Maybe the explosives weren't even real, but it was a chance he couldn't take. He had to stop her from pushing the button.

It wasn't easy.

Annette and he fell to the floor. Hard. So hard that it knocked the breath out of him for a few seconds. Still, he managed to keep hold of her wrist while trying to wrench the trigger from her hand.

But Annette managed to pull another trigger. The one on her gun.

The sound blasted through the barn. The bullet slammed into the ceiling.

She pulled the trigger again. And again. Each shot so close to his ear that it'd be a while before he could clearly hear anything.

And worse.

Seth wasn't sure where those bullets had gone.

Annette fought like a wild animal. Screaming obscenities. Kicking and biting. She clamped her teeth onto his arm, and Seth could have sworn he saw stars.

Still, he held on to her left hand and finally managed to yank the triggering device from her. He couldn't just toss it for fear it'd go off, but he eased it aside so he could try to deal with the woman. He had to be careful, though, not to let the scuffle land them on the button that could blow them to bits.

Part of him wanted to shout out to Jewell, Roy and Shelby to get out of there. Just in case those explosives also were on some kind of timer. But he couldn't do that.

Not with those gunmen outside.

Seth hadn't heard any shots fired in the past couple of minutes, but that didn't mean the hired thugs weren't there waiting to carry out their boss's final orders.

Seth caught the movement behind him and cursed when he spotted Shelby. She was right there. Too close. And Annette was trying her damnedest to aim her gun at Shelby.

Roy came out from cover, too, and aimed his gun at Annette, and Shelby went after the triggering device.

"Don't touch the button," Seth warned her, though she likely already knew what they were dealing with. "But get it away from Annette."

Shelby picked it up as if it was a fragile piece of glass that might shatter in her hands, and she moved it to the tractor seat.

One thing down. Now, to deal with Annette.

Seth bashed the woman's hand against the barn floor, and her gun finally went flying. It landed far enough away for it to be out of her reach.

"You can't do this," Annette cried. The tears returned with a vengeance.

But Seth didn't feel a single grain of sympathy for the woman. She had killed and would have killed again if she'd gotten the chance. He stood and dragged Annette to her feet.

"Should we take off those explosives?" Roy asked.

Seth shook his head. "Annette might have some kind of booby trap device on them."

The woman was crazy enough to have done pretty much anything. That was why Seth holstered his gun so he could take hold of both her hands.

"I got a text from Cooper," Roy told them. "He's all right, but someone put a spike strip on the road that was the same color as the asphalt so he didn't see it in time. He has flat tires, but he's making his way on foot to the ranch. I told him to be careful."

That only seemed to enrage Annette even more, and she started to struggle again. Seth didn't care for slugging a woman, but if she kept it up, that was what he might have to do. He didn't have time to babysit her, not with her two hired guns still out there. Cooper or one of the ranch hands could be shot.

"The fire," Jewell said. "It's destroying the house."

Seth realized then his mother was looking out the barn door at the house. He got to her and motioned for her to step back. "Find something to gag Annette. I don't want her shouting out orders to those thugs."

Shelby quickly took care of that. She ripped off her shirtsleeve and tied it around Annette's mouth. Shelby wasn't especially gentle about it, either, and Seth didn't blame her. Annette had come darn close to killing her. Later, he'd do something to try to soothe the anger and fear he saw in Shelby's eyes, but for now he had to get them to safety.

Seth shoved Annette to her knees. "Put your hands on top of your head," he ordered. "Keep a gun aimed at her," he told Roy once Annette had done that. "If she moves or tries to get away, shoot her. Just don't hit the explosives."

Roy didn't hesitate in taking aim at her, and Seth motioned for Jewell and Shelby to move so he could look outside. He took out his gun, opened the door slowly and listened for any sound that would alert him to the positions of the gunmen.

Nothing.

No one was shooting, but Jewell had been right about the fire. It would soon take down the house. It sickened him to the core to see the damage that Annette's insanity had caused.

He finally spotted Darnell. The ranch hand had taken cover by the front of the detached garage, and Quint was at the back. They both had their guns raised.

"Where are the shooters?" Seth called out to them.

"The one on this side of the house went running off toward the fence," Darnell answered. "I don't know about the other one." Quint verified that with a nod.

Not good. Because the one who'd run could double back, and the other one still could be in place to continue the attack.

"Any sign of Cooper?" Seth asked.

Darnell shook his head. "But some of the other hands went over to Colt's to make sure they were okay and give them some backup."

Good. Because Seth definitely didn't want this

danger headed in the direction of the wives and kids. Since Cooper's wife and son were also at Colt's, that might be where he was going, too.

"Text Cooper," he told Shelby. "I want to find out his location." Because if bullets started flying, Seth didn't want Cooper to get caught in friendly fire.

The wind had carried away most of the tear gas, thank goodness, but the smoke and heat from the fire were still making their way into the barn. Worse, sparks were flying.

Literally.

And if one of those sparks made it to the barn, the fire could spread there. Seth already had too few options and didn't want to lose the cover of the barn.

"Cooper's out in the west pasture making his way here," Shelby relayed. "I told him to be careful and watch for the shooters."

Good.

If Cooper made it there in the next couple of minutes, then they could do something about getting Roy, Shelby and Jewell out of there. Cooper also could arrest Annette. But with the danger from that fire, Seth might have to run to a car and drive it back to the barn for the others. At least he still had the cruiser, and it was bullet resistant.

Of course, there were a good thirty yards

between him and the car. And it might be rigged with explosives.

The detached garage was closer, and there were certainly some vehicles inside, but he didn't want to take the time to hotwire anything, and he wanted as much protection for Shelby and the others as he could get. That meant he'd need to check the cruiser to make sure no one had tampered with it. That'd eat up precious time, too.

Someone fired a shot. Not nearby, but on the west side of the burning house. Seth held his breath. Waiting. And he finally saw Cooper step out.

"The gunman's dead. How many more are there?" Cooper called out.

"I'm not sure. One of them ran away."

Without warning, Annette let out a fierce scream. Somehow, she'd managed to remove the gag, and even though she was still on her knees, she threw her body at Roy, her head bashing into his legs. It was just enough to throw him off balance, and he staggered back.

"I'll kill you all!" Annette shouted, and she tried to claw her way toward Shelby.

The problem was that Annette was so tangled up with Roy that Seth didn't have a good shot. But he couldn't just stand by and let this play out. If Annette managed to get Roy's gun, no doubt she would start shooting.

Roy rolled on top of Annette, trying to get control while she threw punches at him and kicked him. Jewell tried to help. Not a good idea. Because the moment his mother leaned down to latch on to Roy, Annette grabbed Jewell's arm and pulled her into the fray.

Hell. Enough of this. Annette still had those explosives strapped to her, and Seth didn't want them going off.

"Keep your gun aimed at her in case she tries to run, and if she does, shoot her in the head," Seth told Shelby.

It took Seth a moment to find a part of Annette he could reach, and he yanked her by the hair to pull her out of the tangle of bodies. He was succeeding.

Until the gun went off.

Everything seemed to freeze. All except Seth's mind. It was racing with all the bad possibilities. Shelby, Roy or his mother could have been shot.

Roy untangled himself, pulling Jewell out with him.

And that was when Seth saw the blood.

THERE WAS SO much blood on Jewell's shirt that it took Shelby a moment to realize Seth's mother hadn't been hit.

All that blood belonged to Annette.

The woman was flat on her back on the

ground, her left hand sprawled out to the side, her blank eyes fixed on the ceiling.

"Annette grabbed my gun," Roy said, his voice shaky. The rest of him was shaky, too. "She pulled the trigger."

After everything Annette had done, Shelby doubted the woman had meant to kill herself. No. She'd probably been trying to kill Roy or anyone else she could shoot. Thank goodness her sick plan had backfired, and Shelby felt nothing but relief about that.

Roy's phone dinged, indicating he had a text message.

"Cooper," Jewell said. There was so much breath in her voice that Shelby was surprised she could speak. The woman's legs buckled, and Shelby quickly stuffed the gun in the back waistband of her jeans so she could take hold of Jewell.

"Is Cooper okay?" Jewell asked. "What about the others?"

"Cooper's still fine," Roy answered when he read the text. He fired off a reply. "He's going to keep watch, but he's making his way to the barn."

Good. Maybe it wouldn't be long before the firefighters could get on the property, as well.

But Shelby's heart sank when she looked out the door and saw the house. Oh, mercy. The fire was about to bring it down to the ground, and even if the fire department arrived in the next minute or so, there wouldn't be much to save.

"Your home," Shelby said, touching her fingers to her lips.

Jewell made a sound of agreement, but Seth didn't. His attention was back on Annette, and there was such alarm on his face that Shelby looked to make sure the woman hadn't managed to come back to life.

"Did Annette touch the explosives when you were fighting?" Seth asked Roy.

The question caused Shelby's heart to go to her knees. No, please. This couldn't be happening now. Not after everything Annette had put them through.

"Maybe she touched them," Jewell conceded.

Roy nodded in agreement. "Why?"

"Because some of the sticks of explosives have been moved, like maybe they've been shoved apart." Seth went closer, motioning for them to stay back. "Maybe they got moved during the struggle."

Shelby did stay back, but she watched as Seth leaned in and had a closer look at Annette's torso. She wasn't sure how he could see anything with all that blood, but he must have noticed something.

Something that caused Seth to curse.

"Get out of the barn now!" he shouted.

Seth didn't wait for them to do that. He grabbed Shelby and got her moving. Roy did the same to Jewell.

"The explosives are on a timer," Seth told them. "I couldn't see when it's set to go off, but it could be any second."

That got Shelby moving even faster, and Seth hurried them in the direction of the detached garage.

"Run!" Seth shouted to Cooper, and then to Darnell and Quint. The ranch hands took off, heading for the pasture.

Even though they were in a footrace against those explosives, Seth still kept watch around them. For a very good reason. At least one hired gun was still missing, and Annette might have left orders for him to shoot to kill.

The moment they reached the garage, Seth pulled them to the side, and Roy pressed a keypad on the exterior. The heavy doors began to grind open.

But it wasn't soon enough.

The blast ripped through the air, so powerful that it shook the ground.

Shelby didn't have time to react before Seth pulled her to the ground, and, as he'd done before, covered her with his body.

Just as the fiery debris from the barn came raining down in the yard.

Instantly, there was more smoke, more heat, more flames, and some of the debris smacked into the fire-eaten house, causing portions of it to collapse. When Seth started to get up, he had to drop back down again to keep from getting hit.

"Mom?" Seth called out.

Shelby had been certain that Jewell and Roy were right there with them, but she looked around as best she could and didn't see them.

Mercy, had they gotten hit with some of the rubble?

Now that the garage doors were fully open, Shelby could see they weren't inside there, and it certainly didn't help when Jewell didn't answer.

However, Shelby did hear *something*.

"No," Roy said.

Not a shout, but there was certainly enough anger and emotion in his voice for Shelby to know that something else was wrong. But what exactly that was, she couldn't tell. Because she still couldn't see either Jewell or Roy.

Where were they?

"Stay down," Seth told her, and he hurried toward the sound of Roy's voice on the other side of the detached garage.

Shelby didn't move, but she could see the

change in Seth's body language. Every one of his muscles turned rock hard, and he pointed his gun at something.

Or rather *someone*.

Nothing could have stopped her at that point. Shelby still had her gun, and she had to try to help.

She inched her way to the corner of the garage, fully expecting to see Annette's hired thug there, holding his weapon on Jewell and Roy.

But she was wrong.

Partly anyway.

The hired thug was indeed there, his weapon aimed at Seth and Roy. However, someone else had Jewell at gunpoint.

"Shelby," her father said. He even smiled at her. "I'm so glad you're okay and that Annette didn't get to finish what she started."

But her father clearly had plans to finish something.

Whitt had Jewell on her knees, his gun jammed to the back of her head.

Chapter Seventeen

The adrenaline was already slamming into Seth, but now he got another jolt of it. Along with the sickening feeling of dread.

No. This couldn't be happening.

But it was.

Whitt was finally showing exactly what kind of a man he was: a killer.

It hurt Seth too much to see his mother's face. So pale. So afraid. But also ready to die if it meant she could somehow save them.

"Let her go," Roy demanded.

"Right. As if that'll work. Keep watch behind us," Whitt told the hired gun. "And if Roy and Seth don't drop their weapons, kill them. I'd rather they watch while I settle things with Jewell, but I'm not opposed to a change in plans."

Unlike Annette, Whitt didn't seem to be flat-out crazy. Those were the eyes of a man hell-bent on revenge and his warped sense of justice.

Even though Jewell was the one in need of some real justice here.

"Please let Roy, Seth and Shelby go," Jewell begged.

Whitt didn't even spare her a glance. "Drop your guns," the man snapped, volleying his gaze between Seth and Roy.

It took Seth a moment to realize that Whitt hadn't demanded the same of Shelby. That was because she wasn't holding a gun. It was tucked in the back of her jeans, and her hands stayed limp by her sides.

"Dad," Shelby whispered, her voice strained and raw. Like the look on her face. Not shock or disappointment. Something even stronger.

Horror.

"Yeah," Whitt said to her. It sounded like the start of some kind of apology. "I didn't want it to go down this way. Annette went off the deep end and set up this dog and pony show. I'm just cleaning up her mess. That's one of the reasons I came back, to make sure she didn't kill you."

It cut Seth to the bone to see Shelby this way. To see those tears in her eyes. Of course, she'd known her father was a rapist and liar, but she'd probably held out hope that he wasn't also a killer.

"For the record," Whitt added to Shelby. "I never tried to kill you or Seth. *Never*. That was all Annette's insane doing. You're my little girl. My princess. And I'll always love you."

The words sounded perverse coming from Whitt. Did he think he could sway Shelby to his way of thinking? Of course, Shelby was in shock. Perhaps very close to breaking down, so anything might work right now.

"But you did kill someone," Seth tossed out there. He kept an eye on the thug. Kept watch around them, too, in case Whitt had other hired guns nearby. "Marcel."

Seth hadn't been sure his theory was right, but he saw the confirmation spark in Whitt's expression. Annette had confessed she'd murdered the others but not Marcel. In fact, Annette had been upset about his death, and that meant someone else had killed him.

"Marcel," Whitt repeated. "I feel a little bad about that. Annette let something slip to him, and he found out I was alive. Marcel called me. He said I should do the right thing by Jewell so she could get out of jail and that he'd recorded our call to turn over to the sheriff. Of course, he didn't say anything about a recording until near the end of our conversation, or I'd have been more careful with my choice of words."

"I'm guessing you confessed to the rape," Seth threw out there.

Whitt only glared at him. "I mentioned something about wanting Jewell to rot in jail. I wanted her there until it was time for her to get the punishment she deserved for leading me on and then crying rape. No woman rejects me. No. Woman!"

Now Seth could see how Whitt wanted his sick plan to play out.

"So you came back to Sweetwater Springs to get the recording, kill Marcel and stop Annette," Seth said. "You knew your arrival would get Jewell out of jail, but you probably figured that would just make it easier for you to kill her."

"And I don't plan on letting Roy have her," Whitt finished. "Not in this lifetime anyway." He jammed the gun so hard against Jewell's temple that she gasped in pain.

Hell. It took every bit of strength for Seth not to launch himself at the man and tear him to pieces.

"So you're going to kill all of us?" Shelby asked.

Whitt shook his head. "No. Not you. Not even Seth and Roy. They'll live."

It was no doubt Whitt's way of torturing them. If Seth was to believe the man, Roy and he would be alive, but they'd have the nightmarish memories of Jewell dying in front of them.

"I'll have to leave soon," Whitt continued,

talking to Shelby. "And you're more than welcome to come with me."

Shelby swallowed hard, her gaze frozen on her father. "Why are you doing this? *Why?*" Her voice shattered, and the tears came sliding down her cheeks.

"Because Jewell lied. It wasn't rape. She wanted to be with me."

"No," Jewell whispered, but that only caused Whitt to dig the barrel of the gun into her skin.

"You wanted me," Whitt argued. "But then you grew a conscience and called it rape. Well, if you hadn't planned on getting in that bed with me, you wouldn't have come to the cabin."

In Whitt's delusional mind, that probably made sense, but Seth knew the reason Jewell had gone there. To tell Whitt to back off. But Whitt's ego hadn't been able to handle a rejection like that.

"You're the reason I had to leave," Whitt went on, his rage aimed at Jewell. "I couldn't be sure you wouldn't spread that lie around town and have me arrested. I wasn't going to spend one second in jail because of you."

"I didn't want you," Jewell said, "and I didn't tell anyone about the rape until after you came back."

Whitt ignored that and shifted his attention back to Roy. "Last chance. Drop your gun now, or I pull the trigger in three seconds. And I'll change my mind about letting you live and shoot you first." He didn't waste any time starting the countdown. "One, two—"

"I've spent twenty-three years protecting you from this man," Jewell said, her focus on Roy, too. "Don't throw that all away. Please put down your gun."

Roy didn't look at her. He kept his glare on Whitt. Seconds passed. Slowly. Then Roy cursed and tossed his gun to the ground.

"Good boy," Whitt said.

Seth was afraid that patronizing tone was going to cause Roy to snap. While Seth wouldn't blame Roy for doing that, he didn't want anything to spin this further out of control. He had to figure out how to get Whitt's gun away from Jewell and make sure the thug didn't end up killing them all.

"Now it's your turn, Seth. Drop your gun," Whitt ordered.

"I will, but why don't you go ahead and let Roy and Shelby go. They don't need to see this."

"Oh, but Roy does. He needs to see what it's like to lose."

Seth had to get his teeth unclenched before he could continue. "Then, let Shelby go."

"No," Shelby spoke up. "I'm staying." She

wiped away some tears. "Dad, please. Don't do this."

If Whitt had any reaction to that, he didn't show it. He kept his attention nailed to Seth. "Time's up. You should have put down your gun when you had the chance."

And Whitt pulled the trigger.

THE SHOCK HIT Shelby so hard that her vision blurred, and despite the deafening blast from her father's gun, she had no trouble hearing the screams. First, from her own mouth.

And then from Jewell's.

The blood came. Spreading across Jewell's sleeve, and it took Shelby several heart-stopping seconds to realize Whitt hadn't shot Jewell in the head but rather in her arm.

"You bastard!" Roy shouted, and he came at her father.

Roy didn't get far. The hulking hired gun rammed his shoulder into Roy's body and sent Roy straight to the ground. The impact must have knocked the breath from him because Roy started to gasp and wheeze. Shelby wanted to go to him, but the thug shook his head as if he knew what she was considering.

"The next shot will hurt Jewell even worse because it'll go in her gut," Whitt spat out, his venomous eyes aimed at Seth. "Now put down that gun and get Shelby out of here."

When her father looked at her, Shelby thought she might see genuine concern on his face.

Might.

But considering he'd just shot Jewell, Shelby doubted he had any real concern left for anyone. Including her.

Cursing, Seth lurched forward and probably would have thrown himself at her father if Shelby hadn't stopped him. Whitt would shoot him. She had no doubts about that now. And he'd shoot Roy, too. In fact, despite her father's reassurance that he would let everyone but Jewell go, Shelby didn't believe him.

Jewell clamped her teeth over her bottom lip, clearly trying to fight the pain. "Seth, please. Just take Shelby and Roy and leave. It's the only way you'll be safe."

"We'll never be safe as long as Whitt's alive." Seth's voice was low and dangerous.

It was true. But at least if they stayed alive, they'd be able to track down Whitt and bring him to justice. That wouldn't happen if her father managed to kill them all right here.

"Well?" Whitt spat out, looking at Seth again now. "What will it be? I can put bullets in your mother all day if that's what you want. Enough bullets for her to bleed out right in front of you.

Or you can give me what I want and put down the gun."

Think.

She had to do something to stop this.

Then she remembered the gun she'd tucked in the back of her jeans. Her father hadn't seen it. Or if he had, he'd obviously thought she wouldn't use it against him. Shelby would if she thought she could shoot him before he killed one of them. But she knew her aim wasn't nearly good enough to make a tight shot such as that. Not with Jewell and Roy so close.

But Seth could.

Shelby looked at him. "Go ahead. Put down your gun. It's what your mother wants you to do."

She hoped the words were right. Enough to convince her father that she was helping to move his sick plan along. However, Shelby also hoped that Seth knew what she was truly offering.

Her gun. To him.

She didn't want to motion toward the weapon in case her father or his goon noticed, but as observant as Seth was, she had to believe he'd seen it.

"Please, Seth," Jewell added. "Please put it down."

The woman's breath came in jagged bursts now, and she was trembling. No doubt from the blood loss and pain. She needed an ambulance. Roy perhaps did, too, and that was all the more reason to speed this along.

The muscles in Seth's jaw tightened. His neck corded. But he finally dropped his gun on the ground in front of him.

"Get their weapons," her father immediately ordered the other man.

The guy reached to do that, but he stopped and pivoted in the direction of the guesthouse while moving back in front of her father in a protective stance. That was when Shelby saw Cooper. He was armed and leaning out from the exterior wall.

Shelby's first reaction was relief. They obviously needed backup. But this was a very precarious situation right now, and if Cooper starting shooting, it could turn even more deadly than it already was.

"Cooper," Whitt called out. "I know you're not especially fond of your mother, but if you want to be the reason she dies the hard way, then fire your gun. You might hit my friend here, but he's wearing a Kevlar vest."

Shelby didn't see the bulletproof vest, but the guy had on a bulky T-shirt covered by a black nylon jacket. It could be hidden along with other backup weapons. But she was fairly certain that Cooper, too, carried a backup gun. She prayed he did anyway, because it might be necessary if bullets started flying.

"If you don't do as I say," her father added to Cooper, "then Jewell will be the one who pays the price. So throw down your gun, put your hands on top of your head so I can see them and join us."

"Do it, Cooper," Seth insisted. "Put down your gun."

That didn't help Cooper's already stony expression. Seth and he weren't on friendly terms, and Cooper probably thought Seth had lost his mind asking him to surrender his weapon. But the truth was Cooper didn't have a shot. Yes, he could shoot the goon in the head, but by then Jewell would be dead.

Maybe the rest of them, too.

Her father already had his gun in his hand, and he'd proved he had no trouble shooting someone.

Roy glanced at both Seth and Cooper. Then her. Maybe he suspected that Seth and she had a plan, because he maneuvered himself so that he could see Cooper.

"Son, do as they say," Roy insisted. Shelby wasn't sure how he managed to keep his voice so calm with Jewell bleeding and in pain just a few feet away.

Jewell nodded. "Cooper, do it. I don't want any of my children paying for what I did."

That put a smile on Whitt's face. A smile that sickened Shelby so much that she nearly gagged.

"You gotta love a woman who admits she was wrong," Whitt said. And he smacked a kiss on Jewell's pale cheek.

Shelby was terrified that would set off Cooper, Seth and Roy, but Cooper tossed his gun into the yard between the garage and the guesthouse.

"Well done," Whitt proclaimed. "Roy and Jewell, I have to admit you did raise some obedient children."

"I'm obedient," Shelby lied.

Another smile. So much evil. So sick. Yet she couldn't let him see that right now.

"I've missed you," she said to him.

"I missed you, too, princess."

She took a step closer to her father. A move that also put her slightly in front of Seth. Where he'd hopefully have a better chance of reaching her gun. If not, at least she'd be in front of him.

Seth wouldn't care much for that.

But her father had already given this family enough pain. Shelby wasn't going to let her father take Seth from Jewell.

"I need you next to Roy," Seth whispered to her.

Her stomach sank. Because Shelby was almost

certain what Seth was asking her to do. After he pulled her gun, Seth wanted her to drop out of the way so that he would be left to shoot it out with her father and the thug.

If she'd been wrong about Cooper having a backup weapon, then Seth would die.

"You can come with me if you want," Whitt said to her. But then his gaze shifted to Seth. "But you won't. Because you're in love with him. And everything you're saying right now is all to protect him."

It was.

And Whitt must have seen the truth in her eyes because her father whipped his gun right at her.

He was fast.

But Seth was faster.

Shelby barely felt his hand when Seth pulled the gun from her jeans. He fired. Not once, but a double tap of the trigger, and he used his body to push her to the ground. Shelby already had started in that direction anyway, but Roy dragged her down next to him and reached for Jewell.

That was when Shelby heard the other shots.

It all happened at once. A whirlwind of gun blasts, shouts and blood.

The hired gunman froze. Then dropped, his weapon falling right next to him. From the corner of her eye she saw that Cooper had been the one to take him out.

Then Seth fired again.

And Shelby saw her father.

Seth's bullets had gone into his chest and head.

Whitt's smile was gone now. And everything else, too. No life was left in him, even though he was still on his feet.

That only lasted a split second before her father crumpled into a heap on the ground.

Shelby couldn't move. But she certainly could feel. She braced herself for all the raw emotions she thought might come. After all, her father had just died right in front of her eyes. But the only thing she felt was relief.

It was over.

Almost.

"Call an ambulance!" Roy shouted. He scooped Jewell into his arms.

Cooper took care of that, and Shelby got a closer look at Jewell's injury. Not just to her arm as she'd originally thought. The blood had spread across her chest.

Jewell was bleeding out.

Chapter Eighteen

Seth wished he could do something to ease the shock and fear he saw on the faces of all the people in the hospital waiting room.

Rosalie's husband, Austin. Colt, Tucker and their wives, Elise and Laine. Plus, Cooper's wife, Jessa, and Jewell's sister, Kendall, with her fiancé, Aiden, who was also Shelby's brother.

But Seth figured that same look of shock was also on his own face.

The adrenaline had come and gone, leaving him exhausted and a little numb. Not numb enough, though, because whenever the image of Whitt crossed his mind, he got a new jolt of anger. Annette and Whitt had come damn close to killing them all.

And might have succeeded in killing Jewell.

His mother was still in surgery, which meant they were all waiting for the outcome of this nightmare. Waiting for news of Rayanne's labor, too. Too bad waiting wasn't exactly Seth's strong suit. Even the bone-weary fatigue couldn't stop him from pacing.

Unlike Shelby.

With her sister on one side of her, and her brother on the other, Shelby was slumped down in one of the hard plastic chairs, and she was staring at the floor. Seth had tried to comfort her. Multiple times. But the one-word responses and dazed looks she'd kept giving him were enough to let him know she needed some time.

Maybe plenty of time.

Heck, maybe even forever.

After all, she'd watched him gun down and kill her father.

Yes, Whitt had done some bad things. Very bad. But maybe all of that bad couldn't totally kill a daughter's love for a father she'd longed to see for most of her life.

Kendall stood, prompting Aiden to stand, too, and he left his sister's side to go to Kendall's. He pulled her into his arms. Kissed her. Even though they'd been together for well over a month now, it still gave Seth a little jolt. Whitt's son and Jewell's sister together.

Which wasn't a whole lot different from Seth's sleeping with Whitt's daughter.

And they weren't the only ones who'd managed to put this family feud to rest. Since they'd arrived at the emergency room, Tucker had been giving Laine hugs of comfort. And love.

Seth had no trouble seeing the love between them.

And then there was Roy. His face was bruised and battered from his run-ins with Annette and Whitt's thug, but he'd refused medical treatment. He wanted all the doctors focusing on Jewell.

Yeah. Roy was a man in love, too.

Nothing could erase the memories of the past. The hurt. But then apparently nothing could erase that kind of love, either.

Seth heard the footsteps, hoped it was news about his mother, but it was news of a different kind. Cooper came in sporting a bandage on his arm from the injury he'd gotten the day before at the Braddock ranch. It wasn't serious, and it clearly hadn't slowed the man down one bit.

Cooper made a beeline for Seth, and his brothers quickly joined them. "The dead body by the fence is Marvin Hance," Cooper told them.

Seth hadn't realized that Shelby had gotten up from her chair until he heard her make a sound. Part surprise mixed with relief.

"How did he die?" Shelby asked Cooper.

Since she didn't look too steady on her feet, Seth slipped his arm around her. Okay, he did that for himself, too.

Because holding her steadied him.

"We're piecing it together now," Cooper explained. "But judging from some notes found at Annette's place, she was furious with Hance because she thought he was the one who'd killed Marcel."

"But Whitt killed him," Seth quickly pointed out.

Shelby huffed. "My father no doubt convinced her otherwise. That way he didn't have to take the blame for murdering Marcel."

Cooper nodded. "We're also figuring out why Annette took Marcel's death so hard. They've been having an affair for years, and even though Annette was still obsessed with Whitt, she might have been in love with Marcel."

Another example of opposites attracting. The rich city girl and the ranch hand. Too bad Annette hadn't stopped obsessing over Whitt so she could have had a life with Marcel. If she had, none of this might have happened.

Of course, if things hadn't played out like this, his mother might be standing trial—today—for murdering Whitt. It didn't seem fair that Jewell had escaped one injustice only to face another from Whitt's bullet.

Cooper tipped his head to the hall. "Anything about Mom and Rayanne?"

"Nothing yet," Tucker answered.

Seth wondered if Cooper even realized he'd

called her Mom. Any other time it'd been Jewell. So maybe some good had come from this awful situation after all. Not just for Cooper. But for all of them. Despite the fact the room was filled with Braddocks and McKinnons, there wasn't any bad blood.

Maybe because too much blood had been spilled already.

"What about the ranch house?" Colt asked his brother.

"Gone. All of it. There wasn't much the fire department could do by the time they got in there."

Yet another casualty of Whitt's war against the McKinnon's. Since Jewell's father had built the place, it would come as another hard blow.

Colt, Cooper and Tucker stepped away and started a whispered conversation about how they were going to handle the property loss. And the wrap-up of the investigation. Seth figured he should be in on that part of the discussion, but he didn't want to leave Shelby's side, and he didn't want her to have to hear any more details about the destruction her father and Annette had caused.

She looked up at him. No tears. *Now.* However, her eyes were still red. "I'm trying to remember that I loved my father once. I'm trying to hang on to that good part. But it's hard to remember anything good."

That tugged at his heart. To hear the hurt in her voice. To see it in her eyes. Seth brushed a kiss on her forehead.

"Your dad loved you," Seth settled for saying.

Not a lie. In his own way, Whitt had loved her. Probably his other kids, too. He'd just had a warped way of showing it.

"So what now?" she asked.

That was the million-dollar question, and Seth wasn't sure he had a worthy enough answer. Even if he'd had one, he wouldn't have had time to answer, because Rosalie appeared in the doorway of the waiting room. Since she'd been in the delivery room with Rayanne, Seth very much wanted to hear what she had to say.

"It's a boy," she announced. "He's perfect, healthy and screaming his head off right now."

Austin went to Rosalie's side. Kissed her. Smiled, then he kissed her again. In about six months, they'd be doing this themselves, since Seth recently had learned that Rosalie was pregnant.

"Is Rayanne okay?" Roy asked.

Rosalie nodded, gave her father a hug. "The baby weighed eight pounds and five ounces. Rayanne did great. Blue, not so much. He nearly passed out when the doctor asked him to cut the cord."

That caused a trickle of laugher in the room. Blue wasn't exactly the passing-out type.

The relief that his sister was okay hit Seth a little harder than he'd expected. So did the flood of pure joy. His sister was now a mother, and even though Rayanne had a wild streak, he was betting that motherhood would settle nicely on her. Her marriage to Blue certainly had.

"Any news about Mom?" Rosalie asked Seth.

"Not yet."

Roy groaned and scrubbed his hand over his face. "I'll see if I can find out anything." He left the room and headed up the hall.

"I'm so sorry," Shelby said, her voice cracking.

Rosalie blinked. "Please don't think you have to say that for Mom. None of this is your fault, and you don't have to apologize for anything your father did."

Rosalie had taken the words right out of Seth's mouth.

"But I feel so bad, as if nothing I can do will ever make things right." Shelby's tears threatened again, and Seth tightened his grip on her.

"You might feel worse when I tell you I'm in love with you." Seth certainly hadn't intended to blurt that out, and it just hung there, causing the room to go silent.

Shelby turned, slowly. Stared up at him. And her mouth was slightly open. "Why would that make me feel worse?"

Well, hell.

This wasn't a conversation he wanted to have in public with everybody listening, but it seemed a little cowardly to pull Shelby into the corner and talk this out.

"Because you probably don't need a complication like me in your life," Seth said. That had sounded a whole lot better in his head than it did out loud.

"A complication." Shelby repeated it. "Actually, it's a relief. I figured I was going to have to do something huge to make you want to ask me out on a real date. You know, one where we're not getting shot at, burned or blown up."

Shelby somehow managed the impossible. She got Seth to smile. Everybody else in the room did, too.

"Is it true?" she asked. "Are you really in love with me?"

Now Seth pulled her to the other side of the room. Still not much privacy. But he kissed her anyway.

Yeah, he needed that. Needed the feel of her in his arms. The taste of her against his lips. Heck, he just needed her, and Shelby was there for him to take.

When he finally pulled back from the kiss, Seth noticed that most of the people in the room were trying not to stare.

Most.

Aiden's stare was more of a glare, probably because he was wondering what this FBI cowboy was going to do with his kid sister. But Kendall reined in Aiden's glare with a kiss.

Lovebirds.

Until Seth had become one himself, he hadn't known just how good and right it felt.

"It's true," Seth told Shelby. "I'm in love with you." And he waited.

Thankfully, he didn't have to wait long because his heart had seemingly stopped. His breathing, too.

"Good," she said. "Because I'm in love with you. Scary, huh?"

"A good kind of scary," he assured her. A good kind of feeling as well, since it felt as if his heart had doubled in size.

Seth would have finished that off with another kiss, too, if footsteps hadn't grabbed his attention. It was Dr. Howland.

"Jewell's fine," he said right off the bat. "Weak and groggy, but fine."

The good news just kept coming. Maybe because they were due after all the bad news they had gotten lately.

"Roy's with her now in the recovery room," the doctor continued. "I didn't know they were back together, but I for one am glad to see it. Always thought those two were right for each other."

No one in the room disagreed with that—including Cooper, Colt or Tucker. But it did make Seth wonder what Roy had done or what the doctor had seen to make him realize they were back together. Maybe the kissing bug had bitten them, too.

"I can't let you all go in there at once." Dr. Howland's gaze went around the room. "But you can go in two at a time, no more than that, and speak to her for a few seconds. *Seconds*," he emphasized. "Jewell should be plenty well in a week or so, and you'll have time to talk her ears off then."

The doctor motioned for them to follow, and some of Seth's happy mood evaporated. His mother had been through a lot. Maybe too much. And he wasn't sure exactly what he would see when he went into the room.

What he saw was exactly what the doctor had told them. A woman who'd just come through a serious injury, but she still managed to look strong. She smiled when she saw all of them in the doorway.

"Why don't you go first?" Seth offered to Colt, Cooper and Tucker.

"She'd probably rather see you," Colt said.

"She'd rather see all of you, all of *us*," Rosalie corrected. "She loves us all equally, including Seth."

Colt nodded, looked back at his wife. "Then, why don't we go in as couples since the doc said no more than a pair at a time?"

There were sounds of agreement and nods, and Rosalie motioned for Cooper and Jessa to go in. "The eldest son first," Rosalie added when Roy made his way back out to the hall.

Cooper didn't exactly seem comfortable with this visit, but Jessa and he went to Jewell's bed. Seth didn't hear what Jewell said to them, but a moment later, she lifted her uninjured arm and eased them down for a hug.

The relief returned.

"Seth and Shelby, you go next," Rosalie said when Cooper and Jessa started out. "We'll stick with the eldest first because they need to get off their feet faster than the rest of us." She winked at Colt, the youngest of the boys.

Seth was just glad to be included in the visit, but Shelby didn't budge when he started into the room.

"Jewell won't want to see me," Shelby insisted.

"You're wrong," Roy spoke up. "She specifically asked for you."

Shelby went a little pale, but she didn't pull back when Seth led her into the room. Jewell immediately reached out her hand to them.

"I get to see all my kids today and the people who are near and dear to them," she said, her voice hardly more than a whisper. "For a mother, that makes it one of the best days ever."

Seth wasn't sure how she could feel this way after coming so close to being killed.

"I love you," he told his mother, and kissed her cheek.

"I love you, too. And you," she added, looking at Shelby before her attention went back to Seth. "Have you told Shelby you're in love with her?"

There it was again. That mother's sixth sense.

He nodded. "Just now. In the waiting room."

"Not very romantic, but I'm sure you'll make up for that soon." She paused. "The house is gone. I know that. But the way I see it, this is a good thing. Roy and I can build a new place. Have a fresh start. Just like Shelby and you."

There were no tears in his mother's eyes, but Shelby might have some coming on. And there was a darn lump in Seth's throat.

"You don't mind that Roy asked me to marry him again?" his mother said to him.

Seth gave her another kiss on the cheek. "Well, I didn't figure you two would shack up, so marriage is a good starting place."

Jewell smiled. One of those smiles that only a mother could manage. "It's a good starting place for...others, too."

Seth gave her a long look. "Since when did you get into meddling?"

"Since I got shot and know that I can get away with it," she joked. "Seriously, think about that fresh start."

Oh, he would. And Seth also hoped that talk such as that wouldn't send Shelby running in the other direction.

"We have to go," Seth reminded Jewell. "Tucker and Laine are waiting to come in."

He gave her hand a gentle squeeze. Gave her another kiss, and Shelby and he went back into the hall.

"I really like her," Shelby remarked. "She's a very smart woman."

Obviously, Shelby wasn't running, and that actually sounded a little, well, hopeful. Seth decided to test just how hopeful it was.

"Do you want to move in with me?" he asked. "I've got that big house with plenty of room."

Shelby's eyebrows came up, and she took him by the arm and pulled him to the other side of the hall. "You're asking me to live with you because you have a lot of room?"

Finally, here was a question with an easy answer.

"No, I'm asking you because I'm in love with you." Seth reminded her of that with a kiss. One that left them both a little breathless.

But the long, hot kiss didn't take the question out of Shelby's mind.

"All right. So I move in with you? What next?" she asked.

Another easy question. "Lots of kissing and sex."

She laughed, but then quickly put her hand over her mouth to cover it. "And then what?"

Seth thought this answer might be the easiest of all. "Then I ask you to marry me."

He waited, expecting to see that stunned looked in Shelby's eyes.

But it wasn't there.

No tears, either.

Just the same happiness that was causing Seth's heart to feel so full that it might burst.

"I'd rather you ask me to marry you now," Shelby said. "I don't want you to change your mind."

No way would he do that. He wanted Shelby and what he had with her forever.

"Will you marry me?" he asked.

However, before he even got the last word out, Shelby was in his arms. "Yes, yes, yes. I'm more than ready for that fresh start."

So was Seth, and he kissed her.

This was the beginning of their new *forever* together.

* * * * *

Don't miss USA TODAY *bestselling author Delores Fossen's brand new miniseries,* APPALOOSA PASS RANCH, *beginning in November. You'll find the first book,* LONE WOLF LAWMAN, *wherever Harlequin Intrigue books and ebooks are sold!*

Read on for a sneak peek of
LONE RIDER
The next installment in
THE MONTANA HAMILTONS *series*
from New York Times *bestselling author*
B.J. Daniels.
When danger claims her, rescue comes from
the one man she least expects...

CHAPTER ONE

THE MOMENT JACE CALDER saw his sister's face, he feared the worst. His heart sank. Emily, his troubled little sister, had been doing so well since she'd gotten the job at the Sarah Hamilton Foundation in Big Timber, Montana.

"What's wrong?" he asked as he removed his Stetson, pulled up a chair at the Big Timber Java coffee shop and sat down across from her. Tossing his hat on the seat of an adjacent chair, he braced himself for bad news.

Emily blinked her big blue eyes. Even though she was closing in on twenty-five, he often caught glimpses of the girl she'd been. Her pixie cut, once a dark brown like his own hair, was dyed black. From thirteen on, she'd been piercing anything she could. At sixteen she'd begun getting tattoos and drinking. It wasn't until she'd turned seventeen that she'd run away, taken up with a thirty-year-old biker drug-dealer thief and ended up in jail for the first time.

But while Emily still had the tattoos and the piercings, she'd changed after the birth of her daughter, and after snagging this job with Bo Hamilton.

"What's wrong is Bo," his sister said. Bo had insisted her employees at the foundation call her by her first name. "Pretty cool for a boss, huh?" his sister had said at the time. He'd been surprised. That didn't sound like the woman he knew.

But who knew what was in Bo's head lately. Four months ago her mother, Sarah, who everyone believed dead the past twenty-two years, had suddenly shown up out of nowhere. According to what he'd read in the papers, Sarah had no memory of the past twenty-two years.

He'd been worried it would hurt the foundation named for her. Not to mention what a shock it must have been for Bo.

Emily leaned toward him and whispered, "Bo's… She's gone."

"Gone?"

"Before she left Friday, she told me that she would be back by ten this morning. She hasn't shown up, and no one knows where she is."

That *did* sound like the Bo Hamilton he knew. The thought of her kicked up that old ache inside him. He'd been glad when Emily had found a job and moved back to town with her baby girl. But he'd often wished her employer had been anyone but Bo Hamilton—the woman he'd once asked to marry him.

He'd spent the past five years avoiding Bo, which wasn't easy in a county as small as Sweet Grass. Crossing paths with her, even after five years, still hurt. It riled him in a way that only made him mad at himself for letting her get to him after all this time.

"What do you mean, *gone*?" he asked now.

Emily looked pained. "I probably shouldn't be telling you this—"

"Em," he said impatiently. She'd been doing so well at this job, and she'd really turned her life around. He couldn't bear the thought that Bo's disappearance might derail her second chance. Em's three-year-old daughter, Jodie, desperately needed her mom to stay on track.

Leaning closer again, she whispered, "Apparently there are funds missing from the foundation. An auditor's been going over all the records since Friday."

He sat back in surprise. No matter what he thought of Bo, he'd never imagined this. The woman was already rich. She wouldn't need to divert funds…

"And that's not the worst of it," Emily said. "I was told she's on a camping trip in the mountains."

"So, she isn't really gone."

Em waved a hand. "She took her camping gear, saddled up and left Saturday afternoon. Apparently she's the one who called the auditor, so she knew he would be finished and wanting to talk to her this morning!"

Jace considered this news. If Bo really were on the run with the money, wouldn't she take her passport and her SUV as far as the nearest airport? But why would she run at all? He doubted Bo had ever had a problem that her daddy, the senator, hadn't fixed for her. She'd always had a safety net. Unlike him.

He'd been on his own since eighteen. He'd been a senior in high school, struggling to pay the bills, hang on to the ranch and raise his wild kid sister after his parents had been killed in a small plane crash. He'd managed to save the ranch, but he hadn't been equipped to raise Emily and had made his share of mistakes.

A few months ago, his sister had got out of jail and gone to work for Bo. He'd been surprised she'd given Emily a chance. He'd had to readjust his opinion of Bo—but only a little. Now this.

"There has to be an explanation," he said, even though he knew firsthand that Bo often acted impulsively. She did whatever she wanted, damn the world. But now his little sister was part of that world. How could she leave Emily and the rest of the staff at the foundation to face this alone?

"I sure hope everything is all right," his sister said. "Bo is so sweet."

Sweet wasn't a word he would have used to describe her. Sexy in a cowgirl way, yes, since most of the time she dressed in jeans, boots and a Western shirt—all of which accented her very nice curves. Her long, sandy-blond hair was often pulled up in a ponytail or wrestled into a braid that hung over one shoulder. Since her wide green eyes didn't need makeup to give her that girl-next-door look, she seldom wore it.

"I can't believe she wouldn't show up. Something must have happened," Emily said loyally.

He couldn't help being skeptical based on Bo's history. But given Em's concern, he didn't want to add his own kindling to the fire.

"Jace, I just have this bad feeling. You're the best tracker in these parts. I know it's a lot to ask, but would you go find her?"

He almost laughed. Given the bad blood between him and Bo? "I'm the last person—"

"I'm really worried about her. I know she wouldn't run off."

Jace wished *he* knew that. "Look, if you're really that concerned, maybe you should call the sheriff. He can get search and rescue—"

"No," Emily cried. "No one knows what's

going on over at the foundation. We have to keep this quiet. That's why you have to go."

He'd never been able to deny his little sister anything, but this was asking too much.

"Please, Jace."

He swore silently. Maybe he'd get lucky and Bo would return before he even got saddled up. "If you're that worried…" He got to his feet and reached for his hat, telling himself it shouldn't take him long to find Bo if she'd gone up into the Crazies, as the Crazy Mountains were known locally. He'd grown up in those mountains. His father had been an avid hunter who'd taught him everything about mountain survival.

If Bo had gone rogue with the foundation's funds… He hated to think what that would do not only to Emily's job but also to her recovery. She idolized her boss. So did Josie, who was allowed the run of the foundation office.

But finding Bo was one thing. Bringing her back to face the music might be another. He started to say as much to Emily, but she cut him off.

"Oh, Jace, thank you so much. If anyone can find her, it's you."

He smiled at his sister as he set his Stetson firmly on his head and made her a promise. "I'll find Bo Hamilton and bring her back." One way or the other.

CHAPTER TWO

Bo Hamilton rose with the sun, packed up camp and saddled up as a squirrel chattered at her from a nearby pine tree. Overhead, high in the Crazy Mountains, Montana's big, cloudless early summer sky had turned a brilliant blue. The day was already warm. Before she'd left, she'd heard a storm was coming in, but she'd known she'd be out of the mountains long before it hit.

She'd had a devil of a time getting to sleep last night, and after tossing and turning for hours in her sleeping bag, she had finally fallen into a death-like sleep.

But this morning, she'd awakened ready to face whatever would be awaiting her tomorrow back at the office in town. Coming up here in the mountains had been the best thing she could have done. For months she'd been worried and confused as small amounts of money kept disappearing from the foundation.

Then last week, she'd realized that more than

a hundred thousand dollars was gone. She'd been so shocked that she hadn't been able to breathe, let alone think. That's when she'd called in an independent auditor. She just hoped she could find out what had happened to the money before anyone got wind of it—especially her father, Senator Buckmaster Hamilton.

Her stomach roiled at the thought. He'd always been so proud of her for taking over the reins of the foundation that bore her mother's name. All her father needed was another scandal. He was running for the presidency of the United States, something he'd dreamed of for years. Now his daughter was about to go to jail for embezzlement. She could only imagine his disappointment in her—not to mention what it might do to the foundation.

She loved the work the foundation did, helping small businesses in their community. Her father had been worried that she couldn't handle the responsibility. She'd been determined to show him he was wrong. And show herself, as well. She'd grown up a lot in the past five years, and running the foundation had given her a sense of purpose she'd badly needed.

That's why she was anxious to find out the results of the audit now that her head was clear. The mountains always did that for her. Breathing in the fresh air now, she swung up in the saddle, spurred her horse and headed down the trail toward the ranch. She'd camped only a couple of hours back into the mountain, so she still had plenty of time, she thought as she rode. The last thing she wanted was to be late to meet with the auditor.

She'd known for some time that there were… *discrepancies* in foundation funds. A part of her had hoped that it was merely a mistake—that someone would realize he or she had made an error—so she wouldn't have to confront anyone about the slip.

Bo knew how naive that was, but she couldn't bear to think that one of her employees was behind the theft. Yes, her employees were a ragtag bunch. There was Albert Drum, a seventy-two-year-young former banker who worked with the recipients of the foundation loans. Emily Calder, twenty-four, took care of the website, research, communication and marketing. The only other employee was forty-eight-year-old widow Norma Branstetter, who was in charge of fund-raising.

Employees and board members reviewed the applications that came in for financial help. But Bo was the one responsible for the money that came and went through the foundation.

Unfortunately, she trusted her employees so much that she often let them run the place, including dealing with the financial end of things. She hadn't been paying close enough attention. How else could there be unexplained expenditures?

Her father had warned her about the people she hired, saying she had to be careful. But she loved giving jobs to those who desperately needed another chance. Her employees had become a second family to her.

But the thought that one of her employees might be responsible made her sick to her stomach. True, she was a sucker for a hard-luck story. But she trusted the people she'd hired. The thought brought tears to her eyes. They all tried so hard and were so appreciative of their jobs. She refused to believe any one of them would steal from the foundation.

So what had happened to the missing funds?

She hadn't ridden far when her horse nickered and raised his head as if sniffing the wind. Spurring him forward, she continued through the dense trees. The pine boughs sighed in the breeze, releasing the smells of early summer in the mountains she'd grown up with. She loved the Crazy Mountains. She loved them especially at this time of year. They rose from the valley into high snow-capped peaks, the awe-inspiring range running for miles to the north like a mountainous island in a sea of grassy plains.

What she appreciated most about the Crazies

was that a person could get lost in them, she thought. A hunter had done just that last year.

She'd ridden down the ridge some distance, the sun moving across the sky over her head, before she caught the strong smell of smoke. This morning she'd put her campfire out using the creek water nearby. Too much of Montana burned every summer because of lightning storms and careless people, so she'd made sure her fire was extinguished before she'd left.

Now reining in, she spotted the source of the smoke. A small campfire burned below her in the dense trees of a protected gully. She stared down into the camp as smoke curled up. While it wasn't that unusual to stumble across a backpacker this deep in the Crazies, it *was* strange for a camp to be so far off the trail. Also, she didn't see anyone below her on the mountain near the fire. Had whoever camped there failed to put out the fire before leaving?

Bo hesitated, feeling torn because she didn't want to take the time to ride all the way down the mountain to the out-of-the-way camp. Nor did she want to ride into anyone's camp unless necessary.

But if the camper had failed to put out the fire, that was another story.

"Hello?" she called down the mountainside.

A hawk let out a cry overhead, momentarily startling her.

"Hello?" she called again, louder.

No answer. No sign of anyone in the camp.

Bo let out an aggravated sigh and spurred her horse. She had a long ride back and didn't need a detour. But she still had plenty of time if she hurried. As she made her way down into the ravine, she caught glimpses of the camp and the smoking campfire, but nothing else.

The hidden-away camp finally came into view below her. She could see that whoever had camped there hadn't made any effort at all to put out the fire. She looked for horseshoe tracks but saw only boot prints in the dust that led down to the camp.

A quiet seemed to fall over the mountainside. No hawk called out again from high above the trees. No squirrel chattered at her from a pine bough. Even the breeze seemed to have gone silent.

Bo felt a sudden chill as if the sun had gone down—an instant before the man appeared so suddenly from out of the dense darkness of the trees. He grabbed her, yanked her down from the saddle and clamped an arm around her as he shoved the dirty blade of a knife in her face.

"Well, look at you," he said hoarsely against her ear. "Ain't you a sight for sore eyes? Guess it's my lucky day."

JACE HAD JUST knocked at the door when another truck drove up from the direction of the corrals. As Senator Buckmaster Hamilton himself opened the door, he looked past Jace's shoulder. Jace glanced back to see Cooper Barnett climb out of his truck and walk toward them.

Jace turned back around. "I'm Jace Calder," he said, holding out his hand as the senator's gaze shifted to him.

The senator frowned but shook his hand. "I know who you are. I'm just wondering what's got you on my doorstep so early in the morning."

"I'm here about your daughter Bo."

Buckmaster looked to Cooper. "Tell me you aren't here about my daughter Olivia."

Cooper laughed. "My pregnant bride is just fine, thanks."

The senator let out an exaggerated breath and turned his attention back to Jace. "What's this about—" But before he could finish, a tall, elegant blonde woman appeared at his side. Jace recognized Angelina Broadwater Hamilton, the senator's second wife. The rumors about her being kicked out of the house to make way for Buckmaster's first wife weren't true, it seemed.

She put a hand on Buckmaster's arm. "It's the auditor calling from the foundation office. He's looking for Bo. She didn't show up for work today, and there seems to be a problem."

"That's why I'm here," Jace said.

"Me, too," Cooper said, sounding surprised.

"Come in, then," Buckmaster said, waving both men inside. Once he'd closed the big door behind them, he asked, "Now, what's this about Bo?"

"I was just talking to one of the wranglers," Cooper said, jumping in ahead of Jace. "Bo apparently left Saturday afternoon on horseback, saying she'd be back this morning, but she hasn't returned."

"That's what I heard, as well," Jace said, taking the opening. "I need to know where she might have gone."

Both Buckmaster and Cooper looked to him. "You sound as if you're planning to go after her," the senator said.

"I am."

"Why would you do that? I didn't think you two were seeing each other?" Cooper asked like the protective brother-in-law he was.

"We're not," Jace said.

"Wait a minute," the senator said. "You're the one who stood her up for the senior prom. I'll never forget it. My baby cried for weeks."

Jace nodded. "That would be me."

"But you've dated Bo more recently than senior prom," Buckmaster was saying.

"Five years ago," he said. "But that doesn't

have anything to do with this. I have my reasons for wanting to see Bo come back. My sister works at the foundation."

"Why wouldn't Bo come back?" the senator demanded.

Behind him, Angelina made a disparaging sound. "Because there's money missing from the foundation along with your daughter." She looked at Jace. "You said your sister works down there?"

He smiled, seeing that she was clearly judgmental of the "kind of people" Bo had hired to work at the foundation. "My sister doesn't have access to any of the money, if that's what you're worried about." He turned to the senator again. "The auditor is down at the foundation office, trying to sort it out. Bo needs to be there. I thought you might have some idea where she might have gone in the mountains. I thought I'd go find her."

The senator looked to his son-in-law. Cooper shrugged.

"Cooper, you were told she planned to be back Sunday?" her father said. "She probably changed her mind or went too far, not realizing how long it would take her to get back. If she had an appointment today with an auditor, I'm sure she's on her way as we speak."

"Or she's hiding up there and doesn't want to

be found," Angelina quipped from the couch. "If she took that money, she could be miles from here by now." She groaned. "It's always something with your girls, isn't it?"

"I highly doubt Bo has taken off with any foundation money," the senator said and shot his wife a disgruntled look. "Every minor problem isn't a major scandal," he said and sighed, clearly irritated with his wife.

When he and Bo had dated, she'd told him that her stepmother was always quick to blame her and her sisters no matter the situation. As far as Jace could tell, there was no love lost on either side.

"Maybe we should call the sheriff," Cooper said.

Angelina let out a cry. "That's all we need—more negative publicity. It will be bad enough when this gets out. But if search and rescue is called in and the sheriff has to go up there... For all we know, Bo could be meeting someone in those mountains."

Jace hadn't considered she might have an accomplice. "That's why I'm the best person to go after her."

"How do you figure that?" Cooper demanded, giving him a hard look.

"She already doesn't like me, and the feeling is mutual. Maybe you're right and she's hightailing it home as we speak," Jace said. "But whatever's going on with her, I'm going to find her and make sure she gets back."

"You sound pretty confident of that," the senator said sounding almost amused.

"I know these mountains, and I'm not a bad tracker. I'll find her. But that's big country. My search would go faster if I have some idea where she was headed when she left."

"There's a trail to the west of the ranch that connects with the Sweet Grass Creek trail," her father said.

Jace rubbed a hand over his jaw. "That trail forks not far up."

"She usually goes to the first camping spot before the fork," the senator said. "It's only a couple of hours back in. I'm sure she wouldn't go any farther than that. It's along Loco Creek."

"I know that spot," Jace said.

Cooper looked to his father-in-law. "You want me to get some men together and go search for her? That makes more sense than sending—"

Buckmaster shook his head and turned to Jace. "I remember your father. The two of you were volunteers on a search years ago. I was impressed with both of you. I'm putting my money on you finding her if she doesn't turn up on her own. I'll give you 'til sundown."

"Make it twenty-four hours. There's a storm

coming so I plan to be back before it hits. If we're both not back by then, send in the cavalry," he said and with a tip of his hat, headed for the door.

Behind him, he heard Cooper say, "Sending him could be a mistake."

"The cowboy's mistake," Buckmaster said. "I know my daughter. She's on her way back, and she isn't going to like that young man tracking her down. Jace Calder is the one she almost married."

Find out what happens next in
LONE RIDER
by New York Times
bestselling author B.J. Daniels
available August 2015,
wherever HQN Books and ebooks are sold.
www.Harlequin.com